THE WOMAN HE CHOSE

SOME CHOICES LEAVE A SCAR

THE JEWEL FAMILY

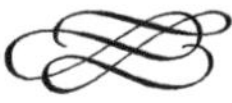

TY'ESHA WILLIS

❀ Formatted with Vellum

This book is dedicated to someone I wish could be here to see this: my mommy, Gail. I miss you every day and hope you are proud of me. Thank you for always being there for me. This one is for you.

CONTENTS

THE WOMAN HE CHOSE

SOME CHOICES LEAVE A SCAR

PROLOGUE

MJ walked past the study on his way to the kitchen and slowed when he heard voices drifting through the cracked door. No one was supposed to be home—not even him.

He'd skipped his piano lesson, deciding video games were a better use of the afternoon, but hunger had sent him on a detour to the kitchen first. He crept closer to the door, careful with each step, straining to hear. Part of him needed to know who was inside. The other part needed to know if they were talking about *him*. Mr. Harris, his piano teacher, never ratted him out as long as MJ didn't miss two sessions in a row—but adults were unpredictable, and MJ trusted none of them completely.

Peering through the narrow opening, he saw his mother standing with her back to him and his father seated behind the desk. The sight alone made MJ's stomach tighten.

This was unusual. Actually—*very* unusual.

His parents barely spoke anymore. They lived in opposite wings of the house—his mother in the west, his father in the east—as if geography alone could keep the peace.

"I know this isn't what you want, Brandy," his father said, his voice firm in a way MJ rarely heard. "But it's happening."

That alone set off alarms. His dad was a lover, not a fighter. He usually went along with whatever his mother wanted, nodding through her endless list of demands just to keep things calm.

"You promised me, Mason," Brandy said, voice harsh. "You promised we would wait until MJ went off to college. You will *not* go back on your word."

"Mason is thirteen," his father said, frustration breaking through. "Tiffany is sixteen, for Goodness's sake. They'll understand."

MJ's breath caught. *We'll understand what?*

"What about the business?" Brandy asked. "We just finished the merger. And the trip we planned with the Taylors—what will people say?"

"There it is," Mason said, standing abruptly. He planted both hands on the desk and leaned forward. "That's the real reason you want to drag this out. We both want out, Brandy. You just don't want to ruin the image."

Her freshly manicured finger jabbed the air between them. "You should care. We are equal partners in this company. This doesn't just upend *our* lives—it rattles shareholders. Sharks will smell blood in the water."

She stepped closer to the desk, her voice dropping, dangerous. "I worked too damn hard for this to let you blow it up."

"Stop being dramatic," Mason said flatly. "It's a divorce. I'm not cutting off your leg."

MJ sucked in a sharp breath, and his elbow brushed the door. *Tap.* His heart slammed against his ribs. His father's head lifted—not toward the door, but toward the floor-length mirror on the wall. His eyes met MJ's reflection instantly. He didn't react. Didn't call him out. Didn't stop the conversation. But MJ knew—without question—that his father had seen him.

Brandy, oblivious, pressed on. "Our name *means something* in this town, Mason. We're stronger together. I told you years ago—you could live your life. Sleep with whoever you want. Come and go as you please. Why are you doing this?"

"Because I'm not happy," Mason whispered. "And neither are you—if you'd stop worrying about how this looks." His voice softened. "You're a beautiful woman, Brandy. We have more money than we could spend in two lifetimes. The business is solid—we just signed an eight-million-dollar government contract for my formula."

MJ's chest tightened. *Eight million.*

"You don't need me anymore," Mason said. "I'll give my shares to the kids. You'll be sole CEO. You were always better at that part anyway."

A heavy silence fell. MJ's heart pounded as he waited for his mother's response.

"Fine," Brandy said coolly. "Give me one day to wrap my head around this. Promise me you won't tell anyone. I'd like to make the announcement, and I'm telling everyone it was my decision."

Mason's eyes flicked to the mirror again, straight to MJ, then back to Brandy. "I promise."

MJ didn't wait to hear more. He slipped away from the door, heart racing, and bolted up the back stairs to his room. His emotions tangled together—fear, excitement, relief. Everything was going to change.

He loved his mother... but he couldn't understand how anyone could love her romantically. She was sharp, demanding, and never satisfied. She complained about everything. When MJ used to tell his dad that his mom was too hard on him and Tiffany, his father always defended her. *She's stressed. The job is hard.*

But MJ couldn't remember a time she *wasn't* like this. She never hugged him after a nightmare. Never kissed his forehead when he felt low. There had been nannies once, but they disappeared when Tiffany turned thirteen. They weren't missed.

Supervision was never an issue—French tutors, debate coaches, tennis instructors, piano teachers. MJ even had football, which his father had fought tooth and nail for. Brandy called it "a waste of time and brain cells." It was the only after-school thing MJ loved. His father had won that battle.

Affection between his parents only existed in public. Cameras on? Brandy clung to Mason like a trophy wife. Behind closed doors, they fought. MJ wasn't surprised by the divorce. If anything, he was relieved.

A knock sounded before his door opened. "Skipping piano again, I see," his father said lightly.

MJ tossed his basketball into the air and caught it, grinning. "It let out early."

Mason laughed. "Sure it did." Then his smile faded as he pulled out MJ's desk chair and sat. "I'm sorry you heard it like that. I wanted to talk to your mother first, then you and Tiffany."

MJ shrugged. "Dad, I'm a teenager. Half my friends' parents are divorced. I figure there'll be more gifts, and I'll keep my cool stuff at your place."

Mason shook his head with a sad smile. "I knew you'd understand. But it's not as fun as you think." He sighed. "You'll have to help your mom more. I won't be here to run interference."

MJ groaned. "Dad, you know how unreasonable she can be."

"I know," Mason said gently. "But it would help me if I knew I wasn't leaving you in the lion's den." He winked. "I'm buying a house nearby. You can come over when she's having one of her bad days."

"All her days are bad!"

"MJ," Mason said in warning. "She's still your mother. You don't have to agree with her, but you *do* have to respect her."

MJ sighed. "Fine. Just buy a house *really* close. Without you here, Tiffany sucking up is going to hit new levels, and Mom's control issues will blow the roof off."

Mason laughed. "Ten minutes. I promise." He checked his watch and stood, pulling MJ into a hug. "Your mom and I have a dinner meeting with Keith. Board stuff." MJ nodded. Keith was brilliant with numbers—almost as good as his dad. "Keith and I will probably watch the game afterward," Mason said at the door. "I'll be home late."

MJ threw the ball up again. "Later, Dad."

Mason paused. "Homework first."

MJ groaned and sat at his desk. He tried to focus, but couldn't. His parents were getting divorced. It didn't shock him, but it scared him anyway. His dad had always been the buffer. The peacekeeper.

Later that night, a knock sounded. MJ opened his door to find Keith—and behind him, Tiffany, crying silently. Panic surged. "Your mom asked me to get you," Keith whispered. "There's been an accident."

"What happened?" MJ asked. "Is Mom okay?"

"She's fine," Keith said. "It's your dad."

When they got to the hospital, everything blurred together. The elevator doors opened, and MJ saw his mother immediately—standing still, expression unreadable. Tiffany ran to her. MJ stayed frozen. His mother said something—quiet, deadly calm. Then Tiffany collapsed, wailing. MJ didn't need to hear the words.

His father was dead.

CHAPTER 1

Mason shot up to a sitting position in bed as remnants of his nightmare faded. Sixteen years later, and that day still played in his dreams; mostly when it was close to a holiday, or sometimes for no reason at all. The loss of his father was a wound that remained open, but most days, he could live and breathe like any other day. Days like this, however, forecasted his mood; he couldn't shake the pain and resentment and guilt the dream brought. Pain at the loss, resentment for his mother who hadn't been in the car with him, and guilt at feeling it should have been his mother, not his father.

They were told his father suffered a heart attack, and that had caused him to crash his car. Mason, who'd stopped going by MJ a few years after his father's death, had been the only one privy to the knowledge that his father was about to file for a divorce; not even his mother knew he was aware. What Mason also knew was that to the outside world, they were the perfect couple, ran a successful business, went to every gala or any place one could be seen. No one knew his father had just finished telling his wife he was divorcing her and there was nothing she could do about it. Mason never even told Tiffany. What good would it do? To everyone on the outside, they were a loving couple. While Brandy was a notorious ball buster, she was known for the love she showed for her family. Perception was everything in this world. Mason wasn't stupid enough to think anything would come from him letting the cat out of the bag but a trip to boarding school.

It was a threat his mother made often when Mason wouldn't bend to her will. To the world, Brandy was a grieving widow; she never remarried, instead taking her lovers on "business trips" and having to "work overnight at the office." To this day, she still wore her wedding ring. She put up the perfect front to the world, but she became even more manipulative than she was before. Without his father there to run interference, Brandy got what she wanted by any means necessary. Football was out of the question, and any friend who wasn't approved by Brandy wasn't allowed over or vice versa. Mason's life was filled with cold, expensive dinners, classes that would look good on a college transcript, and society functions he had to attend with Brandy-approved dates, which were usually her friends' daughters.

Mason missed the warmth his father brought to his life; he let Mason speak his mind, have an opinion. Without his father there, there was no one to stop Tiffany from following in her mother's ridiculously expensive shoes. Tiffany had always wanted her mother's approval, taking on Brandy-approved classes and dates. Expectations were easy for Tiffany. She and Mason got along well enough. It wasn't a close brother-and-sister bond, but as they'd gotten out of the teenage angst, they settled into comfortable communication. It was a source of contempt for Brandy, because while Tiffany was easy to control, Mason was not. He'd taken on his father's fight. To Brandy's frustration, once Mason turned eighteen, she was not in charge of his inheritance and a part of her beloved company. What Brandy and a lot of other people hadn't realized was that Mason Sr. had been trying to take his life back for some time. He'd used their lawyer, much to Brandy's displeasure, to release both children's inheritance at eighteen instead of the twenty-five Brandy had requested. And the last screw you he was able to throw Brandy's way was signing over his forty percent shares to his children two years before his death. This made it impossible for Brandy to get the decision overturned in court, which she had tried a couple of times.

The only time Mason had to see his mother was at board meetings and the obligatory monthly dinners that had also been a request in his father's will. He had a mind to cancel tonight's dinner, but it had been a month since he'd seen his sister too. Tiffany had her eye on taking over for her mother one day, and still molded herself into the perfect Brandy clone, but at the same time plotting to get her mother out well before retirement age.

Brandy kept Tiffany close because her shares often gave Brandy the deciding voice. Mason usually sided with the board, mostly just to piss off his mother. Also because pharmaceuticals weren't his thing. He didn't have a brain for chemistry or formulas like his father. To his dismay, he was very business-savvy like his mother. He'd taken his inheritance and invested in a few companies he'd done his research on, and later opened an import and export company. Mason did very well for himself.

Getting out of bed, he stretched his six-foot-one frame while yawning.

"Leaving so soon?"

Mason turned to the bronze beauty in the bed. "Afraid so, darlin'." He picked up his underwear off the ground and started to dress. "I have a busy day ahead of me, and it starts with me making my flight home."

"You got time for a shower for two?" she asked as she made her way to the bathroom.

He continued to dress, not even a little tempted. "Sorry, I have some calls to make before I hop on my flight." He gave her a kiss and headed for the door.

"Can I call you?"

"That's not how one-night stands work, beautiful." He paused at the door and flashed his pearly whites. "We agreed: no names, no strings. Just me giving you as many orgasms as you can handle." She smiled dreamily. "From that smile, I can tell I held up my end of the deal."

She chuckled. "Hence my reason for wanting to call."

"We'll always have these memories." He smiled and closed the door, heading for the elevator.

* * *

Mason had barely pulled his bags through his front door when his phone rang. He took out his phone to look at the caller ID. Tiffany. He silenced the call and went to grab some juice from the fridge. He sat at his kitchen island drinking his juice and scrolling through emails when he heard his door open, then close.

"Mason?" Tiffany called out.

"In here."

Tiffany walked in and frowned at Mason. "You know you heard me calling you."

"That key is for emergencies only."

"This is an emergency. I called and you didn't answer." She smirked. "I had to make sure you were alright."

"Since I sent you my itinerary, you are well aware I would just be getting home." He finished his juice, threw it in the recycling, then sat back down. "Why are you here, Tiffany?"

She grinned. "Nice to see you too, little monster."

Tiffany was an ebony beauty. They both got their complexions from their mother, but that was all. Tiffany had rich brown eyes, a straight nose, full lips , and a dimple in her chin, and to her mother's envy, naturally long chestnut brown hair. She could have been a model; she had the fashion sense and the size the industry loved so much, but where she fell short was her height. She was only five-two, to her and their mother's dismay. Tiffany tried to make up for it by wearing unreasonably high heels, but even the tallest of heels that she could wear comfortably without toppling over only made her average height. Mason and Tiffany shared all of the same features, it was clear they were related down to the dimple in his chin.

Where Tiffany was short, Brandy was tall, reaching almost five ten and over six feet tall in her heels. She was most women's nightmare; even now, in her late fifties, she was something to behold. She was what they in the business called a manufactured beauty. She had the body of a young model because she paid for it, but her face was untouched and beautiful. Full lips and a nose that looked like it was gifted by a surgeon pulled one's gaze into her naturally hazel eyes. Her hair, though bone straight and butt-length, was bought and replaced on a bi-weekly schedule that made sure no hair on her head was out of place.

Tiffany and Mason weren't close, but they made it a point to check on each other regularly. Ever since they were kids, Tiffany had looked out for herself first, but no one messed with her baby brother except her. Mason felt the same; they got on each other's nerves, but when it mattered, they showed up. He hated how much like their mother Tiffany was; she could be cutthroat and manipulative when the occasion called for it, and sometimes even when it didn't. She had a real eye for business, and unlike their mother, also had a brain for numbers and formulas like their father. She would make a great CEO one day if their mother ever allowed her to take over. Mason was sure that was a long time in the future. His mother would run Jewel Pharmaceuticals until she dropped dead. Tiffany was under the illusion that their mother would see her hard work and her business savvy and just hand over the business any day now, but that was just a carrot she dangled to keep Tiffany under her thumb.

Tiffany had a heart, it was just buried deep down; she hid it very well. Brandy didn't like any show of weakness—Tiffany had learned that from a very early age. She hated her mother's constant ridicule and undermining her at every turn, but to be on top you had to kiss the ring. It was the reason Mason and Tiffany couldn't grow closer. Mason did what was right and treated people with respect. Tiffany didn't give you the time of day if you didn't bring home high six figures, treated staff and co-workers alike as if they all worked for her, and her group of friends were just as stuck up as she was.

"I thought we were all meeting for dinner at seven," Mason asked.

"That's not why I'm here."

"Well, don't keep me in suspense," he said, deadpan.

She huffed. "I just wanted to give you a heads up. Mother invited the Michaels and their children."

The Michaels were a dynasty of luxury hotel owners all over the world. Their "children" were Tiffany and Mason's age and had been the subject of many matchmaking attempts spanning decades. Tiffany had actually dated one of their sons, Dennis, but dumped him when his well-known drug rages resulted in him slapping her. She was shallow and loved the power couple they made, but she was no one's punching bag. Tiffany made him regret ever laying a hand on her, courtesy of her very expensive private self- defense lessons. Mason was proud of his sister and happy he hadn't had to catch a case defending her. Their mother, however, was disappointed that Tiffany didn't just let him sleep it off or get him into rehab. Since that little fiasco, both families had stopped trying to get their children together.

"Why? What's changed?" he asked. Mason was sure something was up; their mother didn't invite guests to dinner unless there was a reason.

Tiffany crossed her arms. "Bella is back, and Dennis is out of rehab."

Mason sat back in his chair and chuckled. "Third time's the charm."

"Fifth time, actually, and don't chuckle too hard. I saw Bella. She's all grown up and gunning for you."

Mason shrugged. "Bella is the least of my worries."

Bella was the Michaels' youngest daughter; last he'd heard, she'd moved away to finish law school. Bella wasn't Mason's type; she wasn't a gold-digging shark like her sister Piper, there just wasn't any chemistry between them, and Mason also made it a personal rule never to date anyone his mother recommended.

"You say that now, little brother, but she's coming to see you."

Mason smirked. "I can take care of myself. Can you say the same?"

Tiffany huffed. "Dennis better sit far away from me if he knows what's good for him."

Mason and Tiffany talked about the dinner scheduled for later, then she left, leaving Mason to think about the drama that lay ahead. His mother and Mrs. Michael were sure to be on the "you need to settle down and start a family" warpath, and truthfully, Mason *was* ready to start his own family, but he would never tell them that. It didn't take a rocket scientist to know he had mommy and daddy issues, he didn't trust easily, and he was extremely rich and good-looking.

Mason wasn't conceited, but he knew he was a catch. Women threw themselves at him, and he was all too happy to catch them. None kept his interest for long, though. They either fell in love too quickly, or thought they could use sex as a tool to string him along. There were too many fish in the sea, and Mason made it clear up front that he was keeping his options open, but women loved a challenge. He just wanted a woman he could trust. He had a lot of money, and he was okay with his future wife spending it, he just didn't want some gold-digger looking to buy every designer item known to man, spending her days by the pool day drinking while the nanny raised the kids. He wanted someone who knew money was just money and your character was more important.

* * *

Mason pulled his mother's chair out and waited for her to sit before taking his own seat.

"The Michaels send their regrets. Bella was feeling under the weather, so they all decided to reschedule," Brandy said. *Good,* Mason thought. Bella didn't want to be thrown at him any more than he wanted to be thrown at her. "You should give her a call and check on her, Mason."

"I'm sure she'll be fine."

"Of course she will, but I'm sure she'd love to hear from you."

"I don't have a medical degree, Mother; I have no reason to call and ask about whatever is wrong with her."

Brandy frowned. "I know that, smartass. I was simply thinking she would like to hear from you."

"I've told you before I'm not interested in Bella. Please stop trying to put us together. It won't work."

"You need to start thinking about settling down. You're thirty. The optics aren't good," she said. Mason looked at Tiffany and rolled his eyes. "I saw that. You know it's true."

"How are things, Mother?" Tiffany asked.

"You'd know if you were in the office this week."

"I haven't taken a vacation in two years, and I was only gone for four days," Tiffany said.

"Ross from Legal hasn't taken a vacation in fifteen years, but you don't see him complaining."

"He also had a heart attack six years ago," Mason said.

"He was right back as soon as he was cleared." Brandy pointed her manicured finger at Tiffany. "That's commitment."

"You're right, Mother. I'm back and refreshed, and I won't be taking off anytime soon."

Mason rolled his eyes again and tried to keep from interjecting. Tiffany would have to find her own backbone. He wasn't going to stand up for her because he knew it would fall on deaf ears. Tiffany was too busy trying to gain their mother's favor, and Brandy never listened to anything that wasn't her idea.

Mason looked through the menu while they talked shop. He was a shareholder but didn't often listen to what they talked about; he looked at the information during the board meeting and voted based on that information. His mother always spun a story to her liking to win people over to her side, but Mason made sure all his decisions were for the good of the company and not his mother. He didn't hate his mother; he just disliked her manipulative nature.

While most children had loving parents who praised them for their good grades, achievements, and were there during times of pain to kiss away the hurt, Brandy had not been that woman. Neither were the nannies she'd hired to raise them. Mason had gotten his love, kindness, and free spirit from his father. He was there for their walks, talks, laughs, and even when Mason was mad at his father for siding with his mother, there was always love.

Brandy didn't love anyone but herself, and she dared anyone to shine a light on her faults. She was good at fixing their problems. Tiffany was arrested but never charged for drug possession when she was a teen, even though she wasn't actually using the drugs, just hanging with girls doing lines. It could have ruined most young black girls' lives, but Tiffany was never charged, or even processed, thanks to Brandy. Mason had run into trouble when he was in college, and a girl looking for a come-up tried to blackmail him with trumped-up sexual assault threats. He didn't hesitate in calling his mother and assuring her he'd never even touched the girl. Not that Brandy cared, Mason could have been guilty as sin, but there was nothing that would mess up the Jewel name. The girl was expelled from school, and Mason never heard from her again. He would have felt bad for her if she wasn't such a bad person.

"Are you listening, Mason?" Brandy asked.

"I wasn't."

"Figures." Brandy rolled her eyes. "I asked if you were bringing a date to the Knight Gala this year."

Mason inwardly sighed; he'd forgotten about the gala. The Knight Gala was an annual party for the who's who of the rich and want to be famous. It also raised millions for whatever charity they were sponsoring that year. What this event did for charity was the only reason he suffered through it. He could just write a check and not attend, but he didn't because the Knights were a great couple—and really good friends of his. Although they were filthy rich, they had hearts; they cared about the world and the people in it. Money just gave them time to mentor. Mason had been one of the beneficiaries of their kindness.

After his father died, Terence Knight was there for Mason. Taking him on as an intern during his summers off from college, Mason learned how to be rich but still keep his soul.

He would support whatever worthy charity they'd chosen, but also to support the Knights. He didn't get to spend a lot of time around Ebony Knight, not as much as he did Terence, but he was around her enough to know she was a nice woman, beautiful inside and out, and loved her family. Mason envied the love that shone in her eyes when she looked at her husband and children. She talked about them with love, respect, and admiration. Mason hoped he ended up with a woman like Ebony.

To his mother, he said, "Yes, I will."

Mason didn't have a date and planned to attend alone, but he didn't want his mother getting any ideas and bringing along someone "he just had to meet." He'd had enough of those setups. Many of those women were beautiful, and some even ended up his bed partner. That is anyone his mother introduced him to would ever be. Once she started talking, he quickly saw why his mother liked them in the first place; they were usually like her or came from money, which was just as good to Brandy.

"Oh, do we know this woman?" Brandy asked.

"I doubt it."

"Well, are you going to tell me her name?"

Mason said the first name that came to mind. "Laura."

"Doesn't ring a bell. What's her last name?"

"There's no need for all that; I'm not marrying the woman. She's just my date."

Brandy sighed aloud and turned her attention back to Tiffany. "Do you have a date for the Knight's Gala?"

The rest of the night went off without a hitch. Mason returned to his house early enough to catch a game. He sat down in his big theater room and opened a beer, sitting on the comfortable recliner his designer picked out. He sighed contently. He made it through another dinner without losing his mind. That was a win in his book.

CHAPTER 2

Jasmine stood outside the Historian, an imposing glass structure that gleamed under the city lights. This was no ordinary hotel; one night here cost more than her monthly mortgage had. She drew in a steadying breath, checked her phone, and sighed when she saw no new messages. Slipping it back into her handbag, she lifted her chin and walked inside.

Heads turned as she crossed the lobby with long, confident strides. At five-eight, she carried herself well, and tonight she had pulled out all the stops. Her off-the-shoulder, floor-length A-line gown clung softly to her curves, a high slit along her right leg revealing smooth, brown butter skin with every step. The silk sage color complemented her cute braids pulled into a bun perfectly.

She smiled and nodded at strangers as she passed, offering warm, easy eye contact. Her makeup looked natural—though it had taken a full forty minutes to perfect. Cool-toned silver shadow highlighted her almond-shaped brown eyes, subtle contour sharpened her nose, nude-brown lipstick defined her full lips, and a dusting of rose warmed her cheeks.

She knew she looked good.

Pausing at the ballroom entrance, Jasmine surveyed the room. The women were stunning—designer gowns worth more than her car, sculpted bodies, surgically perfected faces. She felt a flicker of envy, quickly buried beneath composure. None of it showed on her face. Competition had never intimidated Jasmine. It energized her. She did her best work under pressure. Squaring her shoulders, she brightened her smile and went in search of her target.

She accepted a drink from a passing waiter and drifted toward the silent auction, moving slowly from table to table while scanning the bid sheets. She added her name to a few lists, then lingered beside one display, pretending to admire the items.

A tap landed on her shoulder. She turned, already wearing her winning smile.

"Excuse me, beautiful," a jovial voice said. "I see you're trying to steal my autographed *Ali* playbill. I've been hunting for this thing everywhere." He wiggled his bushy eyebrows. "I play to win."

Amused, Jasmine tilted her head. "Is that right?"

"That's right."

"So if I keep bidding, knowing how badly you want it, that won't bother you?"

His grin faltered as realization dawned. He frowned. "Guess I should've kept my big mouth shut."

Jasmine studied him—late sixties, white beard, wire-rim glasses, round belly stretched beneath suspenders. He looked like a Black Santa Claus. His warmth felt genuine, and her guard lowered. "It's okay," she said. "The autograph's all yours."

"Whew. You had me sweating." He laughed, hands hooking into his suspenders. "Name's Carlton Knight. This is my son's gala. I don't think I've seen you before. You crashing the party?" Jasmine stiffened, but he waved a hand quickly. "Relax, girly. My son's not one of those stuffy suits." He gestured around the room. "Now that you've been seen talking to me, you'll fit right in."

She smiled, tension easing a bit. "Thank you. I was invited—just not originally. A friend got sick last minute."

Carlton waved it off. "All's fair. You helped me with Ali; I helped you with appearances." He winked.

"Thank you, Carlton. You're sweet," she said warmly.

"Isn't he?" a voice cut in. Jasmine hadn't noticed anyone approach. Carlton chuckled as he turned.

"Brandy. Good to see you. Doing some bidding?"

"Surely there's something you want," Brandy replied coolly, ignoring his comment. "You're usually outside smoking cigars."

"Open book I'm afraid," Carlton said, laughing. "Just heading that way now."

"Not before you introduce me to your friend."

Carlton hesitated. Jasmine understood immediately. Brandy Jewel didn't need an introduction. Before the moment could stretch, Jasmine extended her hand. "Jasmine Franklin. Nice to formally meet you, Ms. Jewel."

Brandy didn't take her hand. "Likewise, Ms. Franklin." A pause came. "I'm afraid I don't know who *you* are."

Carlton cleared his throat. "Friend of a friend, Brandy. Claws away." Turning to Jasmine, he added quietly, "She's harmless—just territorial."

"Carlton," Brandy said sharply, "weren't you leaving?"

"Alright, alright. Behave." He leaned toward Jasmine and whispered, "Careful with this one," before walking off.

Brandy studied Jasmine. "You look familiar. Where do I know you from?"

"I interned at Jewel Pharmaceuticals about five years ago."

Brandy's eyes narrowed slightly, searching her memory. "And how was it?"

"Incredible. I learned a lot."

"Good." She turned away.

"Ms. Jewel," Jasmine said quickly, "I've always admired your business acumen. It's why I chose Jewel for my internship. I was wondering if we might do lunch sometime—I'd love to pick your brain."

Brandy smiled thinly. "Call my secretary."

"That's what we call a brush-off," a man said lightly. Mason Jewel stepped up beside his mother.

Brandy chuckled. "Ignore him. My son's a bit of a jokester."

Mason looked from Brandy to Jasmine. "Does she know who your secretary is?"

Brandy scoffed. "If she really wants a meeting, she'll figure it out."

"I will," Jasmine said calmly.

"See?" Brandy smirked and walked away. Jasmine exhaled, energized. Mason Jewel had a reputation—nothing like his mother. Friendly. Brilliant. Rich. A potent combination.

"She's never going to meet with you," Mason whispered. "Susan Terry won't allow it."

"Having her name helps," Jasmine replied. "Thank you."

He raised an eyebrow. "It won't. Susan's a guard dog."

"And you don't think your mother wants to meet me?"

"She couldn't get away fast enough."

"Then maybe I'll pick *your* brain instead," Jasmine said lightly. "I'm Jasmine Franklin by the way."

"I know, I came over to the biding table same time as my mother."

"Ah, so you were ease dropping?"

"Sure was, I've been trying to outbid Carlton all night."

"Let that man have the Ali paybill. He's been looking all over for it."

Mason smiled. "I'm giving it to him for Christmas, I just like to mess with him."

The both stood there smiling for a moment.

"So would it be okay for me to speak with you if I'm unable to get time with your mother?"

Mason smiled. "Are you asking me out?"

"Strictly business."

"First base is off the table then. I only do that on first dates."

She laughed. "Absolutely."

"Dinner's on you."

"It's only right. I'm starting my own accounting firm, and could use advice from a mogul like you."

He handed her a card. "Call my office."

"Is that a line?"

"Call and find out."

She would. As he walked away, Jasmine nearly vibrated with excitement. Mason Jewel—*the* Mason Jewel—had given her his card.

Later, she checked her phone again. Still nothing. At the bar, she positioned herself where she could see Mason without being obvious. His suit clearly cost a small fortune—deep grey fabric that perfectly complemented his ebony skin. The tailored cut hugged his broad shoulders and defined muscles, making it impossible to miss just how fine the man was.He moved easily through the room, surrounded by people, completely at home. She smiled.

She'd made her contacts. She'd been seen. That was enough.

As she turned to leave, her phone buzzed. **Target acquired?**

Jasmine typed back: **Locked in.**

Slipping the phone away, she glanced once more at Mason in the crowd and smiled. Then she left—on her terms.

* * *

Mason watched Jasmine as she exited the ballroom. He was intrigued.

She was beautiful—warm caramel colored skin, curves that caught his attention immediately. If he had to guess, he'd say a C-cup. He was usually a butt man, but Jasmine was more generously blessed up top, and it worked. She wasn't one of those painfully thin, model-types who survived on salads and willpower. She looked like a woman who actually ate food. Mason hated women who lived on diet pills and deprivation.

Her braids were styled into a sleek bun, and Mason was certain she didn't realize that was what made her stand out the most in this crowd. These women wore their hair bone-straight or carefully curated "natural" styles. Braids were considered too urban for these social snobs. He liked that Jasmine clearly didn't care. He liked women who did their own thing.

Her deep brown eyes were guarded, observant—like she was holding something back. A secret, maybe. He couldn't wait to take her out to dinner. He was confident, maybe cocky, but the way she kept checking him out when she thought he wasn't looking told him the interest wasn't one-sided. She intrigued him. If nothing else, he hoped to have found his next bed partner.

She never stayed with one group too long. She checked her phone often but never glanced toward the door like she was waiting for someone. She accepted glasses of champagne from passing waiters but never drank more than a sip before setting them down and moving on. Mason wanted to know more.

"She's a looker, isn't she?" Carlton said, stepping up beside him.

"That she is."

"Did you get her number?"

"Nope." Mason took a sip of his whiskey and coke.

Carlton lifted a brow. "I'm surprised. Did she turn you down?"

"Nope," Mason said with a grin. "I gave her my business card."

Carlton chuckled. "You're a smart man. Still, I'm old-school. I would've asked for her number and courted her properly."

"This isn't your generation, Dad," Terrence said, joining them. "Women can do the chasing too."

"That's right," Mason said, clapping Terrence on the back.

Carlton shook his head, amused. "That's what's wrong with you young folks. The chase is half the fun."

"I'm sure Mason cares more about the *other* half of the fun," Terrence said, wiggling his eyebrows. Mason laughed but didn't respond. He could chase or be chased—it didn't matter. In this case, he wanted to see how Jasmine moved. What she wanted. What her angle was, if she had one.

He was usually good at reading people. Jasmine, though ... she didn't give off the usual signals. She wasn't throwing herself at him, and she wasn't intimidated either. Then again, they'd only spoken for five minutes at a gala where she knew no one. Of course she wanted *something.*

Mason intended to find out what.

* * *

Jasmine slipped into her house and locked the door behind her, leaning her forehead briefly against the cool door. The quiet wrapped around her like a blanket after the constant hum of the gala—no clinking glasses, no curated laughter, no eyes measuring her worth. Just silence and the faint scent of her own perfume.

She kicked off her heels, toes curling in relief against the hardwood floor, and set her evening bag on the console. The sage gown followed a moment later, draped carefully over the back of a chair. Tomorrow, she'd deal with the dry cleaning and the practicalities of real life. Tonight, she wanted one thing.

She grabbed her phone and hit Kiera Green, her best friends name. The line rang once.

"Tell me *everything,*" Kiera said, breathless, as if she'd been waiting with the phone in her hand.

Jasmine laughed softly, padding into the kitchen. "Hello to you too."

"No. Start talking. Did you survive? Did you conquer? Did you seduce a billionaire?"

Jasmine opened the fridge, pulled out a bottle of water, and leaned against the counter. "I survived. I conquered. And"—she paused, smiling despite herself—"I met Mason Jewel."

There was a beat of stunned silence. "Shut. Up." Kiera was a real estate agent and loved to hear about rich people as much as she loved to tour their homes.

"I'm serious."

"No, no, no," Kiera said quickly. "You don't just *meet* Mason Jewel.

You run into his elbow or glimpse him across a room like a rare species. What do you mean you met him?"

"He gave me his card."

A shriek burst through the speaker. Jasmine pulled the phone away from her ear, laughing. "Oh my word. Oh my word," Kiera said. "I knew that dress was a weapon."

"It wasn't just the dress," Jasmine said, calmer now. "He's … different than I expected. Smart. Observant. Not arrogant. And very aware of his mother."

"Which is terrifying," Kiera said. "But still—huge."

Jasmine took a sip of water, her smile softening. "It felt … easy. Like talking to him didn't require armor."

"That's dangerous territory," Kiera said. "Are you forgetting why you went tonight?"

"No," Jasmine whispered. "I didn't forget." She glanced toward the window, city lights blinking back at her. "I got what I needed."

Kiera exhaled. "So your fathers finally going to back off?"

"For now." Jasmine closed her eyes. "I sent him the confirmation before I left. Phone numbers and useless gossip."

"And?"

"I'm so done with him," Jasmine said, voice tight. That earned a pause.

"That's … huge," Kiera said. "You okay?"

"I should feel relieved," Jasmine said. "And part of me does. But part of me hates that it took this to finally get him off my back."

"You did what you had to do to survive," Kiera said firmly. "You don't owe him your peace."

Jasmine swallowed. "Meeting Mason complicated things."

"Because he's real," Kiera said. "And that's his world."

"Exactly." Silence stretched between them, comfortable and knowing.

"So," Kiera said finally, brightening, "are you going to call him?"

Jasmine smiled, slow and thoughtful. "Yes. But not tonight."

"Good," Kiera said. "Let him wonder."

"I plan to."

They talked a little longer—about the gala, Brandy Jewel's brushoff, how nice Carlton Knight was, about how surreal it felt to stand in a room full of power and not feel small. When they finally hung up, Jasmine set her phone down and stood there for a moment, breathing.

Tonight had changed things. She didn't know yet whether Mason Jewel would be friend or foe—but for the first time in a long while, the path ahead felt like it belonged to *her*.

And that was enough.

Jasmine sat down across from her father at Tikka's in mid-town Detroit, the clatter of plates and low hum of conversation doing little to soften the knot in her stomach.

"Why am I here?" she asked flatly.

Jack smiled, wolfish and satisfied, like a man who already knew the answer. "I want details on the gala."

Jasmine snorted. "This could have been a phone call." Jack looked at her expectantly. Jasmine exhaled through her nose. "You said I had to get Karen Marigold's number and any information I could pull from her assistant. He was super chatty—just like you said he would be. I gave you everything he told me. Names, numbers. And as per our deal, I'm done."

Jack leaned back, folding his hands over his chest. "And?"

"And you will no longer involve me in your cons," Jasmine said, her voice steady even as irritation simmered beneath it. "You'll stay out of my life, and my college education is officially bought and paid for. End of story."

Jack chuckled. "I'm a man of my word, Jas. Your debt is cleared." She hated when he called her that. "Did he tell you anything else?"

Jasmine hesitated only a fraction of a second before answering. She told him about the conversation—about the gala, the small talk, the harmless observations. She left out only one detail: that the assistant had asked her out. That she'd declined. Jack didn't need to know that. He'd see it as an opening, another thread to pull, and Jasmine was done being his puppet.

"That's it," she said. "That was the whole conversation."

Jack clapped his hands together, clearly pleased. "Perfect."

Jasmine resisted the urge to scoff. There had been nothing groundbreaking—no vault codes, no house keys, no whispered secrets. Just water-cooler conversation. But Jack had a gift for turning nothing into something, for worming his way into plans that somehow always worked out in his favor. She didn't see the appeal. Selling pieces of your soul for a payoff wasn't worth it. And as far as Jasmine was concerned, Jack's soul had been bought and paid for a long time ago.

"Thanks, Jas," Jack said. "I knew that boy wouldn't be able to resist your beauty."

Her stomach turned. Most fathers wouldn't even think to say something like that—wouldn't dream of using their daughter as bait. "Are we done here?" she asked, already reaching for her purse.

"Why the rush?" Jack said. "I'm working on something big. You sure you don't want in? Could help pay off that house of yours."

Jasmine pulled out a five to cover her soda, but Jack waved it away. "Drinks on me."

She didn't argue. She just wanted to leave. "Thanks, Jack. I've got a meeting to prep for."

He nodded, awkward now, like he was remembering how this was supposed to work. "How's work going?"

Jasmine sighed inwardly. He didn't know. He never did. He didn't know what she did for a living, what she'd studied, didn't even know her house was already paid off, or how hard she'd fought to build a life that didn't orbit his chaos. He checked in once a year—on her birthday—and even that call barely lasted longer than a bad joke.

"Everything's great," she said. "I really have to go. Bye, Jack."

"Bye, Jas."

Jack stood as she did, watching her walk out the door. His smile faded. He wished—sometimes—that he'd been the father she needed. But pretending had never been his strength. Parenthood hadn't been his plan. If it hadn't been for Susan, he never would've let himself be stupid enough to get a woman pregnant.

Susan. That woman had owned him in a way no one else ever had. He'd hated it and loved it all at once. And when she died, a part of him had felt relief—an ugly truth he rarely acknowledged. She'd always tried to bring out the best in him, and if anyone could have made him change, it was her.

When the call came that Susan was gone, it felt like an elephant had settled on his chest. For a while, he thought it might crush him. But grief faded. Perspective shifted. And what remained was a life he could finally shape the way he wanted—along with a daughter who reminded him too much of everything he wasn't. Jasmine had always been self-sufficient. That made it easier to come and go as he pleased. Still, he knew he should've done better. He just hadn't wanted to. She was too much like her mother. Too moral. Too sharp. Too judging.

Jack flagged down the waiter and paid for the drinks. He had plans to finalize, pieces to move. Whatever Jasmine thought, the night had been productive.

And Jack Franklin always knew how to make something out of nothing.

CHAPTER 3

Mason looked up when his office phone rang. "Yes, Sheila?"

"Mr. Jewel, there's a Jasmine Franklin on the line. She says you're expecting her call."

Mason leaned back in his chair and smirked. It was nearly a month since the gala. He'd expected her to call sooner. He had to admit—she'd played it well. "Put her through."

"Yes, Mr. Jewel."

"Ms. Franklin," he said when the line connected. "I'm guessing you didn't manage to get past my mother's secretary."

There was a playful huff on the other end. "Your mother's secretary is worse than a guard dog. She should work for the White House."

Mason chuckled. "I hate to say I told you so—"

"Nobody likes a sore winner, Mr. Jewel."

"It's Mason," he said easily. "And you'll have to get used to it. I like to win."

"I should warn you," Jasmine said, "I'm very competitive. I also like to win."

"Noted." Mason glanced at his watch—three minutes until his next meeting. "So, are you calling to schedule a meeting ... or a dinner?"

There was a pause. "I have a business proposal I'd love your opinion on," she said. "I'm meeting with an investor in two weeks and could really use insight from someone with your background."

"You could always email it," Mason said, testing her.

"I'd rather not risk my work circulating."

"Didn't you say you wanted to open an accounting firm?"

"Yes," she said, then added lamely, "Accounting is very hot right now."

Mason smiled. "Sure it is. I'll have my assistant reach out with availability."

"You're going to ghost me, aren't you?" she teased.

"Hardly. I dream of discussing numbers over free dinner. I'm thinking Italian. Lacey's."

She groaned. "Are you insane? Lacey's is impossible to get into."

"My expertise doesn't come cheap."

She laughed. "Fine. I'll make it work."

"Sheila will handle the logistics," Mason said. "I'm late for a meeting."

"Thank you, Mason."

"Thank me after I read the proposal."

"Fair enough."

* * *

Jasmine looked up from her computer when her phone pinged. She picked it up and couldn't help but smile. A message from Mason's assistant confirmed the dinner reservation—and included Mason's personal cell number, which hadn't been on his business card. That alone felt like a small victory.

She saved his number under his name and sent a quick text confirming Sheila's message. Then, after a brief internal debate, she added:

Just to clarify—this is not a date. This is strictly business.

His reply came less than a minute later.

Sheila is never wrong. Looks like we'll just have to live with it.

Jasmine giggled like a schoolgirl, immediately texting back.

There's a first time for everything. This is a professional business consultation, Mr. Jewel.

This time, his response took longer. Jasmine stared at her screen, suddenly overthinking everything. Had she pushed too hard? Sounded defensive? Flirty? Not flirty enough? She was two seconds from calling Kiera for a sanity check when her phone finally lit up.

I tried to tell her. She's very insistent that I let you kiss me. I don't like disappointing Sheila, so we just won't tell her... unless you actually want to kiss me. In that case—

Jasmine shook her head, laughing softly to herself.

You are ridiculous.

Successful men usually are, he shot back. **Occupational hazard.**

They went back and forth for several more messages—light, teasing, easy. It surprised her how natural it felt, how quickly the conversation slipped into something comfortable and familiar, like they'd known each other longer than a few encounters allowed.

Finally, Mason ended it.

I'll see you at Lacey's. Don't be late.

I'm never late, Jasmine replied. **I'm fashionably punctual.**

I look forward to witnessing this miracle.

Jasmine smiled at her phone long after the screen went dark, then forced herself to refocus on her work. Still, the corners of her mouth kept lifting.

Business consultation or not... something told her this dinner was about to be anything but ordinary.

* * *

"You know watching me won't make me finish any faster," Mason said without looking up.

"I've been pretending to play on my phone for twenty minutes," Jasmine said. "The suspense is killing me."

Mason chuckled and turned a page. They'd met in the lobby—per her *no-date* rule. She'd shown up in a gray suit that hugged her curves despite the professional cut, braids in a bun, and glasses he was certain were purely decorative. Dinner had been effortless. Conversation flowed easily. Mason found himself enjoying it more than expected.

"Are you laughing at me," Jasmine asked, "or my proposal?" Mason laughed again.

Five minutes later, the waiter approached. "Dessert tonight?"

"Yes," Mason said. "Carrot cake."

"Same," Jasmine said, eyes never leaving Mason.

He closed the folder. "This is solid, but your overhead will kill you."

"That's why I need funding."

"Funding only delays the problem. You need clients—fast."

She bristled. "I'm good at what I do."

"I know. But this world runs on names, not resumés. Accountants make good money, but if your looking to break into this world were accountants make more money than some CEO's you'll need to be more than good at what you do. " Her disappointment hit him harder than expected.

"How do I fix that?" she asked.

Mason smiled. "Now *that* is the right question. Auditing would be my first option. People need to make sure their money is being handled properly."

Jasmine agreed. "True. I'm great at forensic auditing."

By the time dessert arrived, Jasmine had reworked half her plan. Mason had saved her time and a lot of money. The waiter set the check next to Mason and left. Jasmine tried to pick it up, but Mason snatched it away. "I told you this was on me."

"And it's cute you really thought I'd let you pay."

"Mason! Don't make me wrestle that check out of your hand. I have to warn you, I know karate," she said, deadpan.

"Seventeen years of Tai Chi. I'd have you on your back before you could blink." His smile was wolfish.

The atmosphere around them shifted as both engaged in a staring contest. Jasmine looked away first and cleared her throat before taking a sip of her water. "You win this round, but don't get used to it."

Mason grinned, took out his card, and flagged down the waiter. "I told you I like to win, Jasmine."

After the check was paid and the business talk officially ended, neither of them made a move to leave. They sat there, lingering over empty plates and half-melted ice in their glasses, the conversation drifting from numbers and strategy to music, travel, and the small, personal details that usually stayed off-limits.

It surprised Jasmine how easy it felt. How natural.

Mason was the one who finally broke the spell—reluctantly.

"I hate to be the responsible adult," he said, glancing at his watch, "but I have an overseas meeting I can't dodge."

Jasmine smiled, masking her own disappointment. "International business. Very glamorous."

"Very annoying," he corrected. "But necessary."

He stood, then hesitated, as if he wasn't quite ready for the night to be over either. "I'm glad you called me, Jasmine. Business proposal or not."

"So am I," she admitted softly.

They walked toward the entrance together, the energy between them shifting—no longer just playful, but charged with something neither of them named.

"I'd like to do this again," Mason said as they reached the door. "Another dinner. One that Sheila doesn't get to label."

Jasmine raised a brow. "And what would you call that?"

He smiled, slow and dangerous. "I'll let you decide."

Her heart skipped, just a little.

"Good luck with your meeting, Mason."

"Thank you, I'll need it. But I'm already looking forward to seeing you again."

As he held the door open for her, Jasmine had the unmistakable feeling that this—whatever this was—was only just beginning.

* * *

Jasmine stared at her computer screen until the numbers blurred together. Columns that normally felt orderly and reassuring now swam in front of her eyes, refusing to settle. She leaned back in her chair and exhaled slowly.

She never had trouble concentrating. Not like this.

Accounting had always made sense to her. Numbers were honest. They didn't flatter, manipulate, or lie to get what they wanted. If you paid attention, they told you exactly where you stood, and she trusted that kind of clarity.

She'd been with Fairbank and Maxwell since graduation, and she loved the work. The complexity of it. The quiet satisfaction of balancing chaos into something clean and logical. Mason's advice had been invaluable—start small, build a reputation, take on auditing clients first. Let the work speak for itself until she could sustain a physical office of her own.

Accountants did make good money. That was the second reason she'd chosen the field. The first was love of numbers. Growing up poor had a way of carving priorities into you. Jasmine didn't want extravagance. She didn't care about galas or glittering rooms filled with people pretending they mattered more than they did. She wanted security.

She'd eaten enough ramen in her life that no amount of trendiness could make her touch it again. She loved living in a house that didn't rely on candles because Jack got distracted and forgot to pay the electric bill. She loved knowing her heat would turn on, her lights would stay lit, and no one could take that from her.

Since graduating, she'd bought and paid off her own house. It was easy to do with no one to care for but herself, and she lived modestly. Not requiring much. She owned her car as well. Every key in her possession was hers—earned, not borrowed. She had no lingering obligations, no strings. Except for the one she'd finally cut.

Jack had paid for her college degree, and even now, the thought made her chest tighten. She would've taken out loans. A hundred loans. A million of them if it meant freedom sooner. But Jack had offered, she'd accepted, and she'd regretted it ever since.

Until now. She was free.

The realization settled into her bones, warm and unfamiliar. Free to live her life without looking over her shoulder. Free to build her business on her own terms. Free to fail or succeed without owing anyone a damn thing. And maybe—just maybe—free to want more.

Her phone buzzed on her desk. Jasmine's heart jumped before she could stop it. She glanced at the screen, half-annoyed at herself for the reaction. *Mason.*

She stared at it for a moment, not wanting to seem too eager. How long should she wait to answer? She then shook her head at how silly she was being and picked up the phone.

I enjoyed our "non-date" and think it would be good to do it again, but this time it's a date so therefore touching me is back on the table. No pressure.

Jasmine chuckled and set it back down, fingers burning to pick it back up. She felt the familiar urge to armor up, to retreat behind caution and control. Mason represented complication. Possibility. A world too close to Jack's for comfort. But he also represented something else: choice.

She picked up her phone, thumb hovering over the screen. For the first time in a long while, the path ahead wasn't being dictated by survival or obligation. She'd been so happy being alone, no one to control her or make her feel like she wasn't important enough to stick around. But Mason had been on her mind almost nonstop since their meeting, and this time, he'd reached out to her!

Mason freaking Jewel had just texted her and asked her out. Picking her phone back up, she stared at his name. Jasmine typed slowly, deliberately. **Hello, Mason. A date-date would be great.**

She set the phone face down on her desk before she could overthink it, a small smile tugging at her lips. Maybe freedom didn't mean isolation. Maybe it meant deciding who earned a place in your life. And for the first time, Jasmine allowed herself to wonder what might happen if she stopped running and started choosing.

Jasmine stared at her phone for exactly three seconds before picking it up again. She didn't overthink this one. She hit Kiera's name and lifted the phone to her ear.

Kiera answered immediately, breathless. "Tell me everything. You never call this early in the day unless something big happened or you're spiraling."

"Mason texted me," Jasmine said.

There was a beat of silence—then a shriek so loud Jasmine had to pull the phone away from her ear. "I *knew it!*" Kiera shouted. "I told you. I told you that man was not letting you walk away. You are that chick!"

Jasmine laughed despite herself. "You're my best friend, of course you think that. But he did ask me out."

Another shriek. Possibly louder.

"Kiera! you are going to make me go deaf."

"Oh my word. Oh my word," Kiera said. "I am living vicariously through you now. You understand that, right? We are both single, but *you* are dating a billionaire. A hot one. This is a civic duty."

"Kiera—"

"Mason Jewel," Kiera said, steamrolling ahead. "*The* Mason Jewel. Do you know how many women would commit light crimes for that man's attention?"

"Slow down," Jasmine said, smiling. "We haven't set any details yet. I literally called you as soon as I texted yes."

"You said *yes*," Kiera repeated, savoring it. "Say it again."

"Yes," Jasmine said, softer this time.

"Okay. First of all, I'm proud of you," Kiera said, her tone shifting just enough to be sincere. "Second—details. What did he say exactly? Where is he taking you? What are you wearing?"

"I don't know," Jasmine said. "That's why I'm calling. I need... guidance."

"Oh, I was born for this moment," Kiera said. "Rule number one: do not treat him like a billionaire."

"I wasn't planning to," Jasmine said.

"Good. Men like that get worshipped or challenged. You? You're neither. You're calm. You're curious. You're the woman who makes him forget he owns half the city."

Jasmine blinked. "That seems ... ambitious."

"Trust me," Kiera said. "Rule number two: ask questions. He's smart. He likes being seen, not studied."

"That actually sounds like him."

"Rule number three: you do *not* overshare. Mystery is your friend. You don't unload your entire life story on date one."

Jasmine hesitated. "What about my dad?"

"Absolutely not," Kiera said firmly. "That's fifth-date trauma at minimum."

Jasmine laughed. "Noted."

"And finally," Kiera said, softer now, "you let yourself enjoy it. No armor. No exit strategy."

"That's the hardest part," Jasmine said quietly.

"I know. But you deserve something easy for once."

Jasmine leaned back in her chair, phone warm against her ear. The nervous energy was still there—but now it was threaded with something else. Anticipation. Hope. "Okay," she said. "I'll try."

"Good," Kiera said. "Because if you don't, I will personally haunt you."

Jasmine smiled. "Thank you."

"Anytime. Now text him back and tell him you're free this week. Preferably somewhere expensive with candles."

"I'll handle it," Jasmine said, laughing. When the call ended, Jasmine stared at her phone again, this time without fear. She didn't know where this would lead, but for the first time, she was looking forward to finding out.

* * *

Mason stared at his phone longer than he cared to admit. That wasn't new. What *was* new was the reason and her name was Jasmine. He wasn't sure what, exactly, had him caught up like this. Attraction alone didn't explain it. He saw beautiful women every day —women polished by money, ambition, and expectation. Women who smiled too quickly, touched too easily, and disappeared just as fast once the novelty wore off. He'd dated rich women, poor women, he was the love them and leave them type. Only a select few could actually say they'd been in an actual relationship with him.

He had never thought twice about a woman once he'd slept with her. Not once. And yet here he was—thinking about Jasmine Franklin. They hadn't even kissed. That fact alone unsettled him. She *was* beautiful, undeniably so, but that wasn't rare in his world. Beauty had become background noise. What lingered was something quieter. The way she listened. The way she spoke without posturing. The way she didn't lean in or pull away—just stood there, entirely herself.

It reminded him of something his father had said once. They'd been sitting in the study late one night. Mason had had another fight with his mother, and he'd asked his father why he'd married her. His father had talked about his mother with love back then. He'd been seven, maybe eight. Not the woman Mason knew now—sharp, calculating, consumed by image and power—but the girl she had been.

"She was quiet," his father had said, staring into nothing. "Beautiful, yes. But honest. She had the kind of heart that made you want to be better just by standing near her."

"What changed?" Mason asked.

His father had sighed like the world weighed a ton. "Money."

His father had come from money. His mother hadn't. They'd met as teenagers, worlds apart, drawn together anyway. Her own father had been abusive—violent in ways Mason's father or mother never detailed. She used to escape to his house, hiding in plain sight. Friendship had come first. Trust. Something gentle.

Back then, his father said, he'd known immediately. *She was the one.*

Mason had never reconciled that story with the woman who raised him. But if he'd learned anything, it was this: money changed people. Power reshaped them. Sometimes beyond recognition. He wondered who his mother might have been without it. And for reasons he didn't fully understand, Jasmine stirred that same quiet curiosity in him. Not urgency. Not conquest. Interest.

Mason shook off the thought and picked up his phone, fingers moving with purpose now. He sent a quick message to his assistant.

Reservation for two at Coats. Friday. 7 p.m.

Coats was trendy without being performative. Italian and Asian fusion, warm, low-lit. A place where conversation mattered more than spectacle. When the confirmation came through minutes later, he didn't hesitate. He opened Jasmine's contact.

Friday at 7 work for you? I've made a reservation at Coats.

It was presumptive, he knew, but she had said yes. And something told him she'd appreciate clarity more than hesitation. The reply came quickly.

Friday works. Looking forward to it.

He smiled before he could stop himself. They exchanged a few more messages—light, easy. A comment about work. A shared laugh over a mutual dislike of small talk. Nothing heavy. Nothing forced. What he noticed most was the pace.

She didn't wait hours to reply. She didn't play games. Her words were frank, honest, and quietly alluring in a way that felt uncalculated. It made him want to know more.

Mason set the phone down, leaning back in his chair, something unfamiliar settling into his chest. Anticipation. Not the kind that came with desire alone—but the kind that came with possibility. And that, more than anything, made him curious about what was coming next.

CHAPTER 4

Mason turned onto Jasmine's street, easing the car to a stop in front of her house. They had been seeing each other pretty regularly for a month now. She lived in a modest downtown Detroit neighborhood—safe, quiet, lined with trees and sun-faded brick. It was a far cry from his marble-and-glass mansion, and he liked that. He liked that she didn't care about the difference.

He checked the mirror one last time—tie straight, collar crisp—then stepped out of the car. Jasmine opened the door before he could knock, smiling like she'd been listening for him.

"Mason," she said, warmth melting across her face. "You're right on time."

"You look ..." He paused, taking her in. She wore a soft green dress that brushed her knees and somehow made her eyes glow. "Incredible."

"And you look incredible as well," she teased, smoothing a hand over his lapel. "As usual."

He laughed. "Just trying to keep up."

"Let me grab my jacket," she said, stepping back inside.

Mason waited at the threshold, hands in his pockets. Something tugged at his attention, though he couldn't place it. He looked around, listening. Nothing. Just the quiet sounds of Jasmine moving inside the house. Still, the hairs on the back of his neck rose. That unease had been happening far too often lately. A moment later she returned, pulling the door closed behind her. "Ready?"

"Yeah," he said, offering his arm. She slipped her hand through his, and for a moment, the world felt simple. They drove deeper downtown toward the restaurant—a small place by the river that Jasmine had picked. Mason liked that about her, too: she chose things that felt personal, not curated for status.

"Long day?" she asked, brushing his hand lightly with her fingertips.

"Not bad," he said. "Meetings. Emails. Avoiding my mother."

Jasmine laughed. "She called again?"

"Twice. I didn't answer."

"Good." She said it lightly, but there was firmness beneath the word.

Mason's mother—who had heard from one of her friends that Mason and Jasmine had been seen together at Lacey's and a few other spots—had been calling nonstop to express her disapproval of Jasmine and her lack of status. Mason was certain his mother didn't realize that her objections only made Jasmine more appealing, not less. He rolled his eyes, remembering the conversation.

Mason had been halfway through reviewing a report when his phone began vibrating. He didn't need to look at the screen to know who it was. He let it ring. Then again. And again. On the fourth call, he'd sighed and answered. "Mother."

"Oh, so *now* you pick up," she'd said sharply. "I was beginning to think you'd blocked me."

Mason closed his eyes. "I'm at work."

"Yet you've still found time to have dinner at Lacey's, Coat's, Levi's and Braiser's," she said. "With *her*."

He leaned back in his chair. "If you're calling to scold me, you're wasting your time."

"Oh, I'm calling to save you from embarrassment," she'd said. "My friends saw you. Jessica could barely wait to tell me all about the *hood girl* my son was parading around like a prize."

Mason's jaw tightened. "Watch your mouth."

"Excuse me?" she said, affronted. "We have a reputation. You can't just be seen out with anyone, Mason. People talk."

"Yes," he replied coolly. "You do."

Her voice sharpened. "If you want to bed her, do it privately. Quietly. Don't turn her into something she isn't."

Mason stood abruptly, chair rolling across the floor. "That's enough."

"You keep taking her out in public," she'd continued, undeterred, "and she—and everyone else—will start believing you're together. Is that what you want? To undo everything we've built for a woman with no standing?"

He'd laughed once, humorless. "You mean a woman who doesn't need standing to be worth my time?" Silence crackled on the line. "I like her," Mason said evenly. "This isn't about sleeping with her."

"That's not how these things work," she said coldly.

"You do know this is super rich coming from someone with a similar working-class family background. You weren't born with money, Mother."

"You're being reckless. Your father and I grew up together. You don't know this girl or her motives."

"No," Mason said. "I'm being honest. I trust Jasmine enough to be able to give her a chance to prove who or what she is truly after. I don't need your help determining who is right for me."

She'd inhaled sharply. "I will not sit by and watch you throw away your future over a girl who—"

"You don't get a vote. You never have. I've never let you dictate who I date, and I'm not starting now."

"You're making a mistake," she said. "And don't expect my support when this ends badly."

Mason was quiet for a moment. "You called me. I don't need your help. And I'm done entertaining this tantrum." Her gasp was sharp, offended. "Goodnight, Mother," he said, and ended the call.

He'd stood there for a moment, phone still in his hand, pulse steady despite the tension humming beneath his skin. His mother's disapproval didn't scare him. If anything, it clarified things. Because for the first time, he wasn't interested in choosing what looked right. He was choosing what *felt* right. And Jasmine—unexpected, grounding, real—was worth every bit of the noise.

Jasmine, however, hadn't been happy to hear what Brandy thought of her. Still, Mason felt it was important she know—especially if she harbored even the faintest sense of hero worship for his mother. He'd warned her about just how cutthroat Brandy could be, and Jasmine's response had surprised him.

"Just so you know she's likely to escalate," he'd said.

"That's fine," Jasmine replied calmly. "But she can't scare me away."

The admission tugged at something deep in Mason's chest. It also strengthened his respect for her.

They reached the river district as dusk spread across the sky, painting the water in muted golds. Mason parked, then walked around to open Jasmine's door. She stepped out, smiling up at him as though the world had narrowed to just the two of them. Then her smile faltered—just slightly.

"What?" he asked.

She hesitated. "Nothing. I just ... thought I saw someone I recognized." She glanced past him toward the sidewalk, then shook her head. "Probably nothing." People wandered the boardwalk. Couples laughed near the water. A man walked his dog. Normal. Ordinary. Jasmine slipped her hand into his. "Come on. I've been looking forward to this."

Mason was more intrigued than ever. That, in itself, felt ridiculous.

Jasmine Franklin didn't demand his attention, didn't disappear for effect, and didn't cling to him like proximity was currency. She existed comfortably in the space between—checking in just enough to feel thoughtful, and giving him room without making distance feel intentional.

She asked how his day was going and actually listened to the answer. She remembered things. Small things. Like how he preferred his coffee, or that meetings past noon made him irritable. When he'd casually mentioned he'd be working through lunch one day, she'd shown up at the hour he said his meeting was ending with a smile and takeout like it was the most natural thing in the world.

He'd been surprised, and so had Sheila, his assistant. She'd been unable to leave because she'd been taking minutes for his meeting. That had done something to him. Mason had leaned back in his chair as Jasmine set the bag down on the small table in his office lounge.

"Please tell me that taste as good as I think it does," he said.

She grinned. "If it doesn't, I'm deeply offended on behalf of the restaurant."

He opened the container and exhaled appreciatively. "You may have just saved my life."

"Dramatic," she'd said, settling into the chair across from him. "But I'll allow it."

They ate for a moment in easy silence, the kind that didn't feel like something waiting to be filled. Mason watched her as she took a sip of her drink, sunlight from the windows casting a glow around her head. He felt cheesy just thinking it.

"You know," he'd said casually, "this sets a dangerous precedent."

She raised an eyebrow. "Me bringing you lunch?"

"Yes," he replied. "I might start expecting it."

She smiled, slow and teasing. "Careful. I don't reward entitlement."

"Noted," he said. "So this was pure generosity?"

"Mostly," she said. "Also curiosity."

"About?"

"How you look when you're buried in work," she said lightly. "Turns out—you're still charming. Slightly grumpier, but charming."

He laughed. "I'll take that."

Their first kiss flashed through his mind uninvited. It had been unhurried, deliberate. Her lips soft, warm, inviting in a way that had stayed with him longer than it should have. It hadn't been rushed or demanding—just enough to leave him wanting more.

"So," Jasmine said, nudging his foot lightly under the table, "are you going to tell me what's got you smiling at your pasta like that?"

"Just thinking," he'd said.

"Dangerous," she teased.

"About how easy this is."

Her expression softened. "Yeah. I was thinking the same thing."

She checked her watch and sighed. "I should let you get back to conquering the business world."

"Already?" he asked.

She stood, leaning in just close enough for her perfume to reach him. "I didn't say I was leaving just yet." She pressed a quick kiss to his cheek—close to his mouth, deliberately so—and straightened, eyes bright with mischief.

"Behave," she said. Mason watched her walk away, a slow smile settling in. Easy, he realized, didn't mean shallow. Sometimes it meant right. And that thought had followed him long after lunch was over.

Mason shifted back into the present as the waiter refilled their glasses, the soft clink of silverware grounding him. Jasmine was across from him, relaxed, eyes bright in the low light of the restaurant. Dinner had been great, and the company even better.

"Work's been relentless lately," Mason said, cutting into what was left of his meal. "A few large projects overlapping. The kind you can't half-focus on without paying for it later. I feel like I need a vacation," Mason said, wiggling his eyebrows.

Jasmine smiled knowingly. "That sounds familiar. I feel like I'm constantly juggling deadlines lately."

"How's building your clientele going?" he asked.

She leaned back slightly, thoughtful. "Slow but steady. Which is fine. I'd rather grow it the right way than rush it."

Mason nodded. "I actually wanted to mention something." He hesitated just long enough to read her expression. "I have a couple of friends who are looking for audits. I gave them your contact information."

Jasmine blinked, surprised. "You did?"

"I did," he said carefully. "But there's no obligation. I just thought it might help get your name in front of the right people."

Her smile softened, grateful—but there was resolve there too. "Thank you. Really. That means a lot. But I need you to know something."

"Okay," he said, attentive.

"I don't want to use your clout to get to the top," she said gently. "I want what I build to be mine. I'm good at what I do—amazing, actually, not to toot my own horn."

He smiled at that. "I don't doubt it for a second."

"But I want my work to speak for itself. If they hire me, great. If they stay, it'll be because I earned it."

Mason reached for his glass, nodding. "That's exactly why I sent them your way. My help ends at the introduction. The rest is blood, sweat, and tears."

She laughed. "Good. Because I was planning on putting in all three."

They lingered a bit longer, talking about small things—travel she wanted to do someday, a project he was quietly proud of, the comfort of finding someone who understood ambition without being consumed by it.

When he walked her to her door later, the night was quiet, the city humming softly behind them. Jasmine turned toward him, keys still in her hand. "Thank you for tonight," she said.

Mason didn't answer with words. He kissed her—slow, intense, unhurried. The kind of kiss that spoke of restraint rather than urgency. Her hands found his jacket, steadying herself as the moment deepened just enough to leave them both breathless.

She pulled back first, smiling softly. "That's all you get tonight."

He chuckled, forehead resting against hers. "I had a feeling."

"More to come," she said, opening her door.

Mason watched her step inside, the door closing gently between them. As he walked back to his car, one thing was clear: this wasn't something he wanted to rush. And for the first time in a long while, waiting felt like part of the reward.

* * *

Jasmine got out of her car and looked around, scanning the quiet street. No familiar faces. The building loomed in front of her—plain brick, dull windows, and a rusted railing along the steps. Nothing special. Nothing threatening. But Jasmine's stomach tightened the moment she saw it. She hated this place. It reminded her of everything she clawed her way out of. A past that refused to stay dead.

Squaring her shoulders, she marched toward the door and punched in the entry code with practiced irritation. The lock clicked, and she walked in. The air smelled exactly the same. With one last look over her shoulder, she stepped inside. The hallway lights hummed overhead, flickering like they always had. Jasmine pressed the elevator button and crossed her arms, the faint buzz in her chest growing louder.

When the elevator arrived, she stepped in and hit the button for the fifth floor. The doors slid shut. And in the seal of that quiet, metal box, she was pulled backward in time.

Her mother's laughter was the first thing she remembered—warm, musical, certain.

Her mother had been a loving woman, the kind of softhearted person who apologized when other people bumped into *her*. She worked two jobs—sometimes three—just to keep their tiny apartment running. Jasmine remembered waking up to the sound of the coffee grinder at four in the morning, her mother humming to keep herself awake.

Her mother was the kind of woman who believed small gestures could hold a broken world together; she packed Jasmine's lunches with handwritten notes even when they couldn't afford the nice snacks; she braided Jasmine's hair each morning, even if she had only gotten three hours of sleep; she worked back-to-back shifts and still managed a smile at dinner, as if love alone could erase the exhaustion.

She didn't raised her voice. Never cursed. Never complained. She loved Jasmine with a ferocity that was gentle but unwavering—a warmth Jasmine mistook for normal. Her mother's biggest flaw was believing people could be healed with enough kindness. Especially Jasmine's father. She remembered watching her collapse into bed after midnight, exhausted but still smiling at Jasmine as if she were the only treasure that mattered. Jasmine had grown up wrapped in love that never wavered.

Susan, Jasmine's mother, was a gentle breeze. Jack, her father, was a windstorm. He loved Jasmine's mother, but only in a way that made sense to him: selfishly, destructively, and never enough. He missed birthdays. Showed up drunk. Left for "business" trips that never brought in money. When he was home, he treated Jasmine like a prop. Not a daughter.

He breezed into their lives like a gust of wind that knocked things over but never stayed long enough to clean the mess. Charming. Slick. Sharp-eyed. A con man through and through. He hustled people at bars, on street corners, in high-end clubs—anyone stupid enough to believe his smile.

Jasmine was eight the first time he used her in a con. She remembered how her mother's face fell when she found out. She remembered the fights. The slammed doors. It was the only time her mother ever raised her voice. The apologies drowned in tears. Yet her mother stayed. Loved him. Believed he'd change. Tried to hold their tiny family together with nothing but hope and tired hands.

And then, the accident.

A freak malfunction at the factory where her mother worked weekends. One moment she was alive and rushing out the door for overtime, and the next, gone. Just like that.

Jasmine remembered the phone call. Remembered how her father punched the wall. Remembered thinking, *I bet he's angrier about losing her income than losing her.* Within months, he disappeared for days at a time. Weeks. He only resurfaced when he needed Jasmine—when a young girl with big eyes and a timid smile could soften his marks.

She learned quickly. Too quickly. How to read people. How to play the role she was assigned. How to answer her teacher's question about her father's whereabouts. How to take care of herself. How to survive a world where the only person who ever truly loved her was dead.

She hated this building because this was where so many of those lessons were carved into her skin. The elevator dinged. Jasmine blinked, her heart hammering, reality flooding back in. The doors opened onto the fifth-floor hallway. Same peeling paint. Same stained carpet. Same ghosts. But she wasn't a frightened girl anymore. She stepped out with quiet confidence, her heels soft against the floor. She was older now. Smarter. Stronger. She'd built herself from the ashes her parents left behind. And she would never —*never*—let her life depend on anyone again. Not love. Not fate. Not luck. Certainly not on a man… no matter how good Mason made her feel.

She steadied her breath and walked toward unit 5C. No weakness. No vulnerability. No more being used. She knocked and waited for the door to open. She whispered under her breath—more promise than prayer: "I won't end up like her."

Jack answered the door quickly, as if he'd been waiting for her. Jasmine eyed him critically. He looked the same. He was still as handsome as ever, now with a little touch of gray; at forty-six, he could still certainly turn heads. Susan and Jack had Jasmine at an early age, both just twenty years old. Jasmine used to think it was the reason for his immaturity, but knew now that was wishful thinking.

"What the hell do you think you're doing?" Jasmine asked as she pushed past him.

"Come in," he said mockingly as he closed the door.

Jasmine stood in the hallway of the apartment with her hands on her hips. "Why are you following us around? I saw you yesterday; you're slipping."

Jack chuckled. "You saw me because I wanted you to. I knew it would get you over here so we could talk."

"We have nothing to talk about."

"I beg to differ. I got you that invite from my friend Meredith, and you in turn have found yourself the girlfriend of one of the wealthiest men in Michigan." His smile was evil.

She frowned. "I got you the information you requested, like you asked."

"Thank you, that information proved useful, but it would seem we have hooked a bigger fish."

"We have nothing! Mason and I have nothing to do with you."

He smirked. "On the contrary, my darling daughter. If you can pull off this score, we'll both be set for life."

Jasmine could feel the steam coming out of her ears. "We will not be doing anything. I am not dating Mason for you."

"You catch yourself liking this guy? You're not ready for a man like him; he would eat you up and spit you out." He pointed a finger at her. "Haven't I taught you anything?"

She rolled her eyes. "Nothing I want to remember."

"Ungrateful." He shook his head. "Listen to me. I know this world. These people cannot be trusted. You need a plan, and I have the perfect one."

Jasmine snorted. "I just bet you do. I'm not interested in your plan. I'm not dating Mason for you, for a plan or some con."

"That so-called con money paid for that fancy degree you got. You owe me, Jas."

"I never asked you to pay for my degree; you offered. It was the least you could do, Jack. I've never asked you for anything, practically raised myself, and covered for you too many times to count."

Jack chuckled, went to the ridge to grab a beer, and then sat in the loveseat in front of the television. Jasmine looked at the apartment she had grown up in. These were the same tan walls, in the same nine hundred square foot apartment. The two-bedroom, one-bathroom place she once loved to walk in and hear her mother singing was now a dark, dungeon-like lair. Jack never opened the shades, so there was only the artificial lighting that did nothing to lighten the oppression this place represented. Standing in the kitchenette, she watched her father open the can of beer and turn the volume on the television up.

"Let yourself out," he said, then took a sip from his beer.

"Stop following him, Jack," Jasmine said before walking toward the door.

"You are setting yourself up for a hard fall; that man doesn't need you. He can have anyone he wants, and you think it's going to be you? That you'll end up fitting the glass slipper and riding into the night? Grow up, Jas!" He was shouting now.

Jasmine just listened, her heart filling with equal parts anger and pain. He was probably right, but she wouldn't give him the satisfaction of knowing he was voicing her own internal fears. Squaring her shoulders, she opened the door and stepped outside into the hallway. This was Jack's world, and he could have it, but he'd better leave hers alone.

* * *

Jasmine sat back from her desk. She was having a hard time concentrating. Her father's words echoed in her head. Her pulse thudded in her ears, drowning out the echo of Jack's last words—*Grow up, Jas!*—like a drumbeat she couldn't turn off. She closed her eyes, inhaled, and let the cool air settle her shaking hands.

He was wrong. And God, he was right.

Mason Jewel lived in a world she'd only ever seen through the wrong end of a telescope—glittering, distant, unreachable. A world where luxury cars were weekend toys and vacations were decided hours before takeoff. A world where people didn't worry about rent or groceries or whether their shoes scuffed because they were the only pair they owned.

And then there was her.

She wasn't supposed to want someone like him, not really.

Wanting him felt like leaning too far over a balcony: thrilling, terrifying, and one mistake away from a fatal drop. She hadn't thought past their business dinner. His business advice had been all she was looking for, but his playful, easy-going manner surprised her. People with his type of money were usually jerks. He was kind, witty, and so damn fine.

She wanted him. More than she could admit. And because she wanted him, she couldn't afford to lose the one safe thing she had left —herself. She took one more steadying breath before pushing away from her desk. Now was a good as time as any to go to lunch. She needed distance. Time. Space to think of something other than the way Mason looked at her like she was the only water left on earth.

But when she rounded the corner, there he was. As if summoned. Mason was stepping out of the elevator, one hand in his perfectly tailored black suit pocket. His hair and beard looked freshly cut. His expression softened the second he saw her, those brown eyes warming in a way that made her chest throb.

"Hey," he said. "I was just about to come to find you." Her throat tightened. *Of course you were,* she thought. She'd completely forgotten their lunch date. Mason didn't forget anything and always showed up —until the day he wouldn't. "Everything okay?"

"Yeah," she lied quickly. "Just need some air."

His gaze searched hers like he could see every unspoken word she was trying to bury. She hated how easily he did that—saw through her, reached into her even when she didn't want to be reached. "Jasmine," he said quietly, "I can tell something's wrong."

Nothing in his voice was demanding. Nothing in his posture hinted that he was angry or impatient. If anything, Mason looked … worried. For her. That made her chest ache even worse.

"I'm fine," she said, backing away half a step. "You don't have to—"

"Care?" he finished for her. She stiffened. He closed the distance between them by an inch. "Because I do."

Jasmine swallowed hard, fighting the sting behind her eyes. This was exactly what scared her—how easy it would be to fall for him completely. And how hard the landing would be when reality eventually returned to collect its debt. "Mason," she whispered, "you don't understand."

"Then explain it to me."

Looking around, Jasmine thought it better to have this conversation anywhere but here. Taking his hand, she led him to the stairway, not wanting to wait for the elevator. Once they got to the bottom, out the door and out in the open, she started down the street. "Walk with me."

Mason let her go a block away from her job before stopping her and turning her slightly to face him. "Talk to me."

She looked away, searching the ground for an answer she never wanted to say out loud. "Guys like you … you don't stay with girls like me."

"Jasmine?" His voice was confused.

"You come from money. From status. From people who don't have to worry about anything except which charity gala to attend. I can't compete with that. One day, someone better is going to walk into the room and you'll realize that I'm just—"

"Stop." His fingers brushed hers, a feather-light touch that grounded her. "Please."

Jasmine almost pulled her hand back on instinct. Not because she didn't want him touching her—she did—but because she refused to be the girl who fell apart just because a man whispered *please*.

She steadied her shoulders. "Mason, I'm not some fragile thing you have to handle like it'll break. I'm fine."

His brow lifted, the smallest, frustrated smile tugging at the corner of his mouth. "I know you're fine. I've never once doubted your strength." His voice softened. "But that doesn't mean you have to pretend you're made of stone when something is hurting you."

She scoffed, crossing her arms. "I'm not pretending. I just don't want to depend on someone who could walk away whenever he gets bored."

Mason inhaled sharply. There it was—the truth she'd been trying to bury. The fear she refused to let own her, even while it chewed at her in the dark. "So that's what this is," he murmured. "You think the money means I'll go looking for someone shinier if you stop being … perfect, fun, my play thing?"

She flinched, barely. He caught it anyway. "I never said that," she muttered.

"You didn't have to."

She hated how easily he read her. Hated and secretly loved it. "I'm not doubting *you*, Mason." Her voice came out low but steady. "I'm doubting the world you come from. People like you—people with power, options—they don't have to stay. I don't want to lose myself waiting for you to decide I'm not enough."

Mason took a slow step closer. Not crowding her. Not cornering her. Just anchoring her. "Jasmine … your independence is one of the first things I noticed about you. You don't bend for anyone. You don't orbit around anything but your own damn gravity." His expression tightened with quiet intensity. "That's why I'm here. Not because you need me. But because you don't."

Her throat tightened, but she didn't look away.

"But I need you to understand something too," he continued. "Me having money doesn't make me invincible. It doesn't buy me immunity from screwing up. I can't promise you a perfect life. I can't promise I'll never hurt you." He hesitated, the honesty sharpening his tone. "And you can't promise not to hurt me."

Jasmine felt that like a punch—because it was true, and she respected the hell out of him for not selling her a fairytale. He exhaled slowly. "Life doesn't hand out guarantees. Not even to people with more zeroes in their bank accounts than sense."

She gave a humorless laugh. "So what, we're both supposed to just … take a leap and hope we don't face-plant?"

"Pretty much," he said with a crooked smile. "Every choice we make is a leap. The only difference is whether you jump with someone you trust or someone you don't."

She looked at him then—really looked. At the man, not the money.

Not the reputation. Not the life he came from. He wasn't promising her a fairy tale. He wasn't promising her safety. He was promising honesty. And space. And the choice to stay or go without pressure. She breathed in slowly. "I don't want to depend on you," she said. "But... I might want you. And that scares the hell out of me."

Mason's voice dropped to a softer, steadier place. "I'm scared too. But I still choose you. And you get to choose me—or not. That's all I'm asking."

Jasmine swallowed hard. Her independence was a shield, yes, but maybe it didn't have to be a cage. "We'll probably screw this up."

"Probably," Mason said, gently taking her hand again. "But I'd rather screw it up with you than play it safe with anyone else."

This time, she didn't pull away.

CHAPTER 5

They hadn't discussed titles. Yet Jasmine felt like they'd be together forever instead of a couple of months. It was just… time. Time spent lingering over coffee long after the cups went cold. Time walking through the city with no destination. That was the thing that kept catching Jasmine off guard.

Men in her past had wanted something—access, advantage, proximity to what she could provide, what she knew, or what laid between her legs. Mason wanted *presence*. He showed up. He listened. When she talked about her work, her plans to build something of her own, he didn't interrupt with solutions or offers. He asked questions. Encouraged her. Trusted her to figure it out.

One evening, Mason invited her to a fundraiser—small, tasteful, the kind of event where money hummed under every conversation like background noise. Jasmine almost declined. But Mason had said, "You don't have to be anything there. Just be with me."

So she went. They were barely inside when a woman glided toward them, her smile practiced, her eyes sharp. "Mason Jewel," she said warmly. "I was hoping I'd see you." Jasmine felt it immediately—the history. The ease. The confidence of someone who already knew where she stood.

"This is Evelyn Hart," Mason said, his hand settling at the small of Jasmine's back without hesitation. "Evelyn, this is Jasmine."

Evelyn's gaze flicked over Jasmine—quick, assessing—before returning to Mason. "Your mother didn't mention you were bringing a guest."

Mason's jaw tightened almost imperceptibly. "My mother doesn't get a calendar of my life."

Evelyn laughed lightly, unfazed. "Still stubborn. I always liked that about you."

Always liked.

They fell into conversation easily—*too* easily. Evelyn talked about old memories, shared acquaintances, and how Brandy had asked after her just recently. She spoke of compatibility without using the word, of legacy and alignment, of how some people simply *fit*. Finally, she turned directly to Jasmine. "Mason, your friend here is very pretty, very wholesome."

Jasmine held her gaze, unflinching. "Thank you, you're very pretty as well. Haven't I seen you in a music video before?"

Mason's lips twitched. Evelyn smiled, but there was steel beneath it. "I wish; that does sound like fun. Unfortunately, I only run one of the world's largest cruise lines with my family. It's why Mason and our family used to be so close. His mother and I still are very close."

"That," Mason said calmly, "is exactly why this never worked." Evelyn blinked. "You aligned yourself with my mother more than me." His voice was steady but final. "You thought proximity to her meant proximity to me. It didn't, and it still doesn't. If you will excuse us, I'd like to show Jasmine around."

Taking Jasmine's hand, Mason walked away. For the rest of the night, Mason and Jasmine had a nice time. Mason sang her praises as an accountant, and whenever he had to step away or someone took his attention, he always got back to her as soon as possible. He made sure she was a part of the conversation and didn't let anyone exclude her. This wasn't her world, but she didn't feel like an outsider.

Jasmine held her own. She was funny, quick-witted, and spoke about politics and business with an ease that turned heads. People leaned in when she talked, genuinely listening. It was clear—she wasn't just beautiful. She was intelligent, confident, and fully in her element.

Mason watched her with quiet pride.

This was the woman on his arm. The woman who fit into his world without shrinking herself to do it.

As the gala began to wind down, the crowd thinned and the music softened. Mason finally pulled Jasmine onto the dance floor, grateful for the chance to have her to himself. He wasn't much of a dancer—never had been—but with Jasmine in his arms, it felt natural. Easy.

She rested her hands on his shoulders, and he held her close, swaying slowly as if the rest of the room no longer existed.

"I didn't scare anyone, did I?" she teased softly.

Mason smiled down at her. "You impressed them. There's a difference."

"I'm glad," she said. "I wasn't about to play small for anyone."

"And you shouldn't," he said firmly. "Ever."

He was glad she hadn't let Evelyn—or anyone else—steal her confidence or ruin the night. Jasmine had her own backbone, her own strength, and he loved that about her. Loved that she didn't need saving. Loved that she stood tall on her own.

As they moved together, Mason realized something with absolute clarity.

This wasn't just a date.This wasn't just chemistry.

This was the beginning of something that was going to change both of their lives.

And for the first time in a long time... Mason Jewel wasn't afraid of that at all.

Later, in the quiet of Mason's house, the city glowing beyond the windows, Jasmine finally spoke.

She studied him. "So that's what mother-approved looks like?"

Mason chuckled. "And that should tell you everything about why she isn't the one."

Something in Jasmine cracked open then—not painfully, but softly. A door she'd kept bolted out of habit. "I'm not easy. I don't come with guarantees."

Mason stepped closer. "Neither do I. I'm not offering permanence or protection. Just honesty. And space. And the choice to walk away if you need to."

Her breath hitched. "I don't share."

"Neither do I."

"You don't have to... I want you."

His voice dropped. "I want you too."

The kiss that followed wasn't rushed. It was exploratory, deliberate —Mason's hands warm and sure, never claiming more than she offered. When they reached the bedroom, he paused, resting his forehead against hers. "Tell me if you want me to stop."

She pulled him closer instead. Their bodies learned each other slowly, a language of sighs and soft sounds, of trust built in inches. Mason treated her like something precious but powerful, worshipful without being possessive. When she gasped his name, it felt like an offering rather than a surrender.

After, they lay tangled together, the city humming beyond the glass. Jasmine traced idle patterns on his chest. "I think," she said quietly, "you might be the man I've been looking for."

Mason kissed the top of her head. "Good. Because I've been looking for you too."

This time, when he held her, she didn't wonder what it would cost. She just let herself stay.

* * *

For the next couple of months, things were beautiful. A dream, really. Dining in, no need for playing dress up every night and being seen at every trendy restaurant. Intellectual conversations on everything from politics to TV shows. Jasmine actually preferred to stay in. Mason was well known and loved.

Everywhere they went, the attention followed him, as it always did —women who knew his name, his face, his wealth. Mason ignored them completely, but Jasmine noticed. And the voice of her father crept in: *Men like him don't stay faithful. Men like him don't marry women like you.*

As if conjuring up the devil himself, Jack called. His voice slipped easily into manipulation, talking about alliances, leverage, and "the Jewel fortune." When Jasmine refused, his tone hardened. "I can expose you," he said. "Who you really are. What we did. Think he'd want you then?"

Jasmine gripped the pen in her hand, her jaw tightening. "You lie all the time, Jack. But you've never lied to me. Not about this. You didn't want to be my father—and I accepted that. We came to an understanding. We were done. So why are you talking like this, going back on your word?"

There was a sharp exhale on the other end. "You sure are protective of this man," Jack said coldly. "He doesn't love you, Jas. And he never will. These rich types don't know what love is."

Jasmine let out a bitter laugh. "That's rich coming from you. You for sure don't know what love is."

Her voice shook now, but she didn't stop.

"You didn't love me. You never have. And regardless of whether Mason loves me or not, I have never been the conning type. You are not going to turn me into your protégé. I don't want your life. I don't want your schemes. I just want you out of mine—like you promised."

Silence.

The kind that made her pulse pound in her ears.

Then Jack spoke again, softer—but more dangerous. "I am protecting you."

"No," Jasmine snapped. "You're trying to control me."

"I'm trying to get you to see how this ends," he shot back. "Do you want to end up a single mother? A trophy wife? While he's out there with women in every zip code?"

Her eyes burned. "Don't you dare project your broken life onto me."

"He's just like the rest of them—"

"No," she cut in. "He's not like you."

That landed.

Jasmine swallowed hard, forcing the words out. "Please. For once in your life—be a father and protect me the right way. Go away. Don't come back. Don't call me. Don't show up. Let me live my life."

Jack was quiet again. Longer this time.

When he finally spoke, his voice was tight. "You're making a mistake."

"Maybe," Jasmine said. "But it will be my mistake to make. Not yours."

"I will leave you alone, but don't come to me once you blow up your life. Your name won't be any good in this city once he'd done with you." Jack warmed. "You'll wish you listened to me."

Something inside her snapped. "Jack, you've been nothing but a scheming, no-good hustler. Where has that gotten you? Have you made it rich and forgot to clue me in?" She laughed. "You clearly aren't anything on your own, so you think you can use me to do what you never could?"

"Your fancy edu—"

Jasmine cut him off. "Shut up! I am sick of you throwing that in my face. I don't owe you anything. I deserve to be happy, Jack. If you come near me or Mason again, you'll regret it, this I promise you." Hanging up, she vowed not to let her father or anyone else ruin what she had with Mason. She would protect what they had at all costs.

* * *

Mason opened the door to find Miles 'Tank' Oliver already smiling like he owned the place.

"About time," Tank said, stepping inside without waiting to be invited. "I was starting to think billionaire privilege meant you didn't have to answer doors."

Mason smirked, closing it behind him. "It means I don't have to answer *most* doors."

They moved comfortably through the space, the familiarity of years settling in without effort. Tank dropped onto the couch like he'd done it a thousand times before, stretching out and surveying the room. "Still minimalist," he said. "You ever going to admit you actually live here?"

Mason poured them both a drink. "I prefer clean, and I believe my designer did a great job not cluttering the place up."

Tank raised his glass. "You did always hate clutter."

They'd met in college, in a business ethics class they'd both despised. The irony hadn't been lost on either of them. Mason had been quiet, already guarded. Tank had been loud, unimpressed, and entirely uninterested in pretending he wasn't there because his father expected it. Tank's family didn't have Jewel money, but they were comfortable. His father was a well-known plastic surgeon—respected, precise, and emotionally unavailable in a way Mason recognized immediately.

They'd bonded quickly. Not over privilege, but over the weight of expectation. The moment that sealed it came late one night during their sophomore year. A group project had imploded, deadlines looming, tempers high. Mason had been calm on the surface, but something inside him cracked when he'd gotten a call from his mother—sharp words, sharper demands.

Tank had watched him hang up and quietly say, "You okay?"

Mason hadn't been. Not even close. They'd ended up on the roof of the dorm building, legs dangling over the edge, beers between them. Mason had finally admitted what he never said out loud—that money made people feel entitled, that love came with conditions, that being "the Jewel heir" was not something he was interested in.

Tank had listened. Then he'd told Mason about his own father—how success was praised, but softness was weakness. How perfection was expected, not earned. "Guess we're both projects," Tank had said, clinking his bottle against Mason's. Something had settled between them that night. Not pity. Not competition. Understanding.

Back in the present. They sent sometime catching up, planning their next basketball game and just hanging out.

Tank took a sip of his drink and studied Mason over the rim of his glass. "You look… different."

Mason raised an eyebrow. "That's vague."

"Yeah," Tank said slowly. "But I don't miss much. It usually takes a couple of beers before you take off the business and mergers face." Mason chuckled. "You still dating Jasmine or some other honey got you all relaxed?"

Mason leaned back against the loveseat, a small smile tugging at his mouth. "Yeah," he said. "Jasmine and I are still going strong."

Tank didn't need an explanation. He'd known Mason long enough —and well enough—to recognize the shift the moment he walked in. Mason looked … lighter. Less coiled. The sharp edges smoothed by something steady and good. Tank took it in quietly. "Well," he said, shifting on the couch, "this confirms it."

Mason glanced over. "Confirms what?"

"Jasmine has your nose open wide," Tank said. "You don't look like a man fighting himself anymore."

Mason huffed a soft laugh took a sip from his drink. "I didn't realize I was that obvious."

"You are to me," Tank replied. "Happy looks different on you bro."

Mason considered that, then nodded. "I am happy. And Jasmine is a big part of that."

Tank's expression softened. "Weighty words from you, my man. You don't say that lightly."

"No," Mason whispered. "I never have." He stared into his glass for a moment. "I've never had a woman make me feel the way she does. Not even close." Tank didn't push. He didn't need to.

Mason's mind drifted—uninvited but welcome—to the night everything changed. It had started like all their other movie nights.

Comfortable. Familiar. Jasmine had cooked—something simple but perfect—and they'd ended up on her couch, legs tangled, watching a comedy neither of them was really paying attention to. They'd gotten into a debate about who was funnier—Kevin Hart or Mike Epps.

"Kevin Hart," Jasmine had said.

"Mike Epps. The delivery alone—"

"You're biased," she'd said, laughing.

"And you're wrong."

He'd made some comment about Mike Epps's facial expressions, reenacting it badly, and Jasmine had laughed so hard she'd leaned into him, breathless and glowing. And somewhere between laughter and quiet, the air had shifted.

The kiss hadn't been rushed. It had been deep. Unavoidable. Like they'd both finally stopped pretending they didn't feel it coming. Her hands had slid into his shirt, and his mouth had found hers again, slower this time, more certain.

Jasmine had pulled back just long enough to take his hand. "Come with me," she'd said softly.

He had. What followed hadn't been hurried or careless. It had been intense, connected, and consuming—the kind of closeness that erased time. Mason remembered thinking, *this is what I was holding back for, this was love.* He remembered waking up with her still curled against him, sunlight spilling across the room, her fingers tracing lazy patterns on his arm. He'd convinced her—barely—to call off work. "I'm not done with you," he'd murmured. She'd smiled and stayed.

Back in the present, Tank watched Mason closely. "You're gone," he said. "Where'd you just go?"

Mason smiled to himself. "Somewhere good."

Tank nodded once. "Yeah. I figured." He lifted his glass. "Just don't forget—good things make noise. People will notice."

Mason's smile faded only slightly. "I know."

Tank didn't say anything for a long moment. He just watched Mason, the way only someone who had known you in your worst seasons was allowed to. Then he leaned forward, elbows on his knees.

"Alright," he said quietly. "Here's the part you're not thinking about yet."

Mason looked over. "Here we go."

Tank snorted. "Don't act surprised. You don't glow like this without consequences."

Mason took a slow sip of his drink. "Go on."

"You're not just dating her," Tank said. "You're choosing her. And that means the world you come from is going to notice." Mason's jaw tightened slightly. "Your mother already has. Your board will, too. Your friends' wives. The charity circuit. Every bored person with money and time will decide Jasmine is suddenly their business."

"I know," Mason said. "And I don't care."

Tank held up a hand. "I'm not saying you should. I'm saying *she* might."

That landed heavier.

Tank went on, measured but firm. "You're used to pressure. You were raised in it. But Jasmine? She didn't sign up for being evaluated every time she walks into a room with you. She didn't grow up learning how to smile through judgment or turn insults into polite conversation."

"She's stronger than you think. She went toe to toe with Evelyn," Mason said immediately. "It was a thing of beauty."

"I believe that," Tank replied. "But strength doesn't mean it won't cost her something."

Mason leaned back, staring at the ceiling. He'd thought about the money. The gossip. His mother's inevitable campaign. But he hadn't fully thought about the quiet moments—the way eyes would linger on Jasmine a second too long, the assumptions, the whispers dressed up as concern.

Tank softened his tone. "I'm not trying to scare you. I'm telling you this because I've never seen you like this. And if you're serious—really serious—then what comes next is protecting her without smothering her. Standing beside her without pulling her into your shadow."

Mason exhaled slowly. "I don't want to be another thing she has to survive."

"Then don't be," Tank said. "Be the place she can breathe."

Mason nodded once, resolute. "Thanks for the advice man."

Tank smiled, satisfied. "Anytime. Don't mess it up. It's the good ones that are unforgiving. I learned that the hard way." He stood, clapping Mason on the shoulder. "Just remember—this isn't a fling. This is the part where life tests whether you mean what you feel." Tank paused near the door, fingers curling briefly against the wood as if he were steadying himself. Mason recognized the look before the words came. "Do you think about her sometimes," Mason asked.

Tank said quietly. "More than I'd like to admit."

Mason nodded. He remembered. Everyone did. "She was good for you. Better than good."

Tank huffed out a breath. "That obvious, huh?"

"She grounded you. And she didn't put up with your bullshit."

That earned a soft, sad laugh. "Yeah," Tank said. "She saw me. Before the restaurants. Before the investments. Before I figured out how to turn the arrogance off and confidence on."

Mason crossed his arms. "You were young back then."

Tank pointed at him. "Stupid. It's okay to call it stupid."

"You cheated," Mason said, not unkindly.

Tank didn't flinch. "I did. Thought she'd yell, cry, and forgive me eventually. Thought she was a constant."

"She wasn't."

"No. She packed up her things and walked out like she'd already mourned me. Didn't look back. Didn't leave the door cracked."

Mason remembered the aftermath—Tank drinking too much, sleeping less, pretending everything was fine. "You were a wreck."

Tank shrugged. "Still am, if I'm honest. That kind of loss doesn't close. It just ... settles." He straightened, the familiar smirk creeping in. "So I leaned into the bachelor thing. Easier to make it a brand than admit I already lost my person."

Mason watched him closely. "But you never let anyone get close enough to replace her."

Tank's smile faded. "Because there is no replacing her." Silence stretched, heavy but not uncomfortable.

"You always end up in the kitchen," Mason said finally.

Tank brightened a little. "That's the one place I don't screw things up. Food is great. You give it attention, respect, time—it rewards you."

"Your dad still hates that."

"Oh, absolutely," Tank said, laughing. "Plastic surgeon dynasty and I'm over here perfecting risotto. But Coats and Lacey's are thriving because I run them smart—even if my heart lives behind the stove." He sobered, eyes locking onto Mason's. "That's why I'm saying this to you. I watched you with Jasmine. I haven't seen you like this—ever. Don't take her for granted the way I did."

Mason's response was immediate. "I won't."

Tank nodded once getting up to leave. "Good. Because losing the right woman when you knew better?" He shook his head. "That's a regret that never shuts up."

He opened the door, then paused. "Don't let the world ruin something good."

When he left, Mason stayed where he was, thinking of Jasmine—and knowing with absolute certainty that he would protect what he'd found.

CHAPTER 6

Mason didn't notice the shift at first. It came quietly, in the way Jasmine lingered longer when they said goodbye, in how her laughter softened into something more private, meant just for him. Mason the man, not the money or status. What he did notice was how right it felt—natural, steady, real. Whatever doubts he'd once had faded, replaced by the certainty that this wasn't just another relationship drifting along on charm and convenience. He wasn't bored, and when she called, he didn't pretend to be busy. He'd once stepped out of a meeting to take her call and see how her review of a client's books went. He actually cared about the things she did. It was new to him; he felt like he was living in a Ne-Yo song.

Brandy noticed too. She'd had her people watching them from a careful distance. Mason was just doing this to piss her off. Every polite suggestion, every subtle warning she'd offered Mason had slid off him without effect. Jasmine wasn't going anywhere—and that was unacceptable. If Brandy couldn't scare her off, she would outmaneuver her. She picked up her phone, already planning her next move.

Brandy Jewel watched the city from her study window, the lights below glittering like a kingdom that had once obeyed her without question. Mason's defiance still echoed in her chest, sharp and unwelcome. He had never liked her methods—not really. Even as a boy, he'd seen through her polish, her carefully curated concern. He tolerated her now. Nothing more.

That hadn't always been the case. Her gaze softened as an old memory surfaced—uninvited and unwelcome. Mason had been seventeen. Still awkward in his height, still unsure of where he fit in a world that expected him to rule it someday. His father had always been better at this. He hadn't said a word at first. Just stood in the doorway of her study, hands shoved into his pockets.

"They're calling you arrogant," Brandy had said without looking up from her paperwork. "You know that, don't you?"

Mason had shrugged. "I didn't do anything."

"I know," she'd replied. And she had. For once, she'd known exactly what had happened—board members' sons threatened by a Jewel heir who refused to bow. She'd closed the folder and looked at him then. Really looked. "You don't need to be liked. You need to be respected. And sometimes respect looks like loneliness."

He'd frowned, confused. "That sounds ... awful."

Brandy had smiled—genuine, not strategic. "It can be. But it also means no one gets to decide who you are but you." For a brief, rare moment, Mason had relaxed. Sat across from her. Asked questions. Listened.

That night, they'd talked for hours—about business, about power, about not letting the world dictate your path. She'd thought, foolishly, that maybe they understood each other. That maybe she'd done something right.

The memory fractured under the weight of the present. Mason wasn't seventeen anymore. And he didn't see her as a protector—only a threat. Brandy's expression hardened as she turned back to her desk. She'd tried reason. Subtlety. Maternal concern. None of it had worked. Every polite suggestion she'd offered had slid off Mason without effect. He didn't argue. He didn't negotiate. He simply refused. And Jasmine Franklin remained.

Brandy picked up her phone. If Mason wouldn't be managed, then Jasmine would be removed. She dialed a number she hadn't used in years.

"Mrs. Jewel," the man answered. "I wondered when you'd call again."

"I need discretion," Brandy said coolly.

"You always do."

"I want a comprehensive background investigation. Jasmine Franklin."

"Connection?"

"My son," Brandy replied, irritation creeping in. "And no—he won't cooperate."

"Understood. Scope?"

"Everything," Brandy said. "Family. Finances. Education. Relationships. Past mistakes. Hidden ones."

"And if there's nothing there?"

Brandy's lips curved, sharp and humorless. "Then you find someone willing to create something. Everyone has a price. Everyone has a crack."

A pause came. "You're looking for leverage."

"I'm looking for inevitability," Brandy said. "Mason doesn't like my methods. He never has. But he understands consequences." She rose, pacing slowly. "He thinks this woman is different. That she's worth defying me for."

"How quickly do you need this?"

"Before he makes her permanent. Before he convinces himself that love is stronger than legacy." She ended the call and stared out into the night once more. Mason had once trusted her judgment. Had once listened. Now he saw her as something to escape. Brandy's fingers tightened around her glass. Everyone thought they understood her—until they were standing in the wreckage she'd so carefully arranged.

* * *

Brandy chose the restaurant with care—quiet, discreet, the kind of place where conversations stayed where they were spoken. Evelyn was already seated when Brandy arrived, poised and polished, every inch the woman who had once fit effortlessly into the Jewel orbit.

"Brandy," Evelyn said, rising to greet her. "Stunning as always."

"Likewise," Brandy replied, air-kissing her cheek before sitting. "You look beautiful."

Evelyn smiled faintly. "Old habits."

They ordered—wine for Brandy, sparkling water for Evelyn—and exchanged pleasantries until Brandy guided the conversation where she wanted it to go.

"I heard you ran into Mason recently," Brandy said, her tone casual.

Evelyn let out a quiet laugh. "At the Metcalf gala."

Brandy's eyes sharpened. "And?"

"He was with this dreadful woman," Evelyn said.

Brandy's mouth tightened. "Of course."

"She didn't blend," Evelyn continued carefully. "She stood out. Which I suppose was the point."

"Standing out isn't always a virtue," Brandy said coolly.

Evelyn hesitated. "I made a joke—nothing cruel—and she said I looked like a girl from an old music video. Crop top energy."

Brandy scoffed. "Classless."

"Of course, she was trying to insult me but didn't even come close," Evelyn said with a huff. "Mason just stood there, smirking."

Brandy shook her head. "Unacceptable. Mason should know better than to encourage that kind of behavior." That detail lingered unpleasantly between them. "You always knew how to carry yourself. You understood the expectations. The optics."

Evelyn's smile faltered. "That's why you liked me."

"And still do," Brandy replied smoothly. "Frankly, Mason would be far better off with someone like you."

Evelyn looked down at her glass. "I could arrange another run-in. If you think it would help. We still attend the same functions."

"No, we mustn't look desperate. He will never return."

Evelyn kept her smile in place as Brandy spoke, nodding at the appropriate moments, but her mind was somewhere else—two years back, replaying scenes she pretended no longer mattered.

She missed Mason. Not just the access, or the ease of being with him, but the way he had once looked at her like she was enough. Before Brandy's voice had crept into every corner of their relationship. Before *optics* became more important than connection.

Brandy had been relentless then. *Mason likes this better. You should ask him to take you here. Bella's is a great place to be seen—mention it casually.*

The suggestions never stopped. Evelyn had gotten used to it. Her own mother had raised her the same way—life as a chessboard, men as pieces to be guided, nudged, positioned. Evelyn had assumed Mason would play along eventually.

She'd been wrong. The memory came back sharp and fast. She'd been giddy that day, practically buzzing. They'd been together six months—long enough for plans to feel real. She'd already imagined the society wedding of the century, the tasteful spread in *Vogue,* the children raised by the nannies she'd researched meticulously.

That afternoon, she'd asked him to come to a mixer thrown by her office. "Wear the Valentino," she'd said lightly. "The navy one. You know—the one I love." Then, almost as an after thought she said: "Oh —and your mom and I are having lunch tomorrow. She wants to talk about my dress for the Halston wedding."

Mason had stopped walking. He'd turned to her slowly, studying her face like he was seeing it for the first time—not after six months of dates, intimacy, and shared mornings. "I don't see a future with you," he'd said bluntly.

The words had hit harder than a slap ever could have. She'd laughed at first. A reflex. "What are you talking about?"

He hadn't raised his voice. Hadn't been cruel. That almost made it worse. "This," he'd said, gesturing between them. "It's not what I want."

She'd screamed then. Every carefully cultivated piece of her composure shattered. She'd listed all the reasons he was wrong—her beauty, her money, her connections, her devotion. She'd told him she was every man's dream. He'd listened, then ended it anyway. She'd left shaking, called her mother first, sobbing until the edges dulled. Then she'd called Brandy.

Brandy had been shocked—*shocked*—but certain Mason would come around. "He always does," she'd said confidently. That had been two years ago.

Evelyn snapped back to the present as Brandy finished speaking, her tone sharp with disdain about Jasmine Franklin. Evelyn smiled automatically, though something twisted in her chest. She missed what she and Mason had before it went wrong. Missed the certainty. Missed the life she'd already planned. And if anyone could help her reclaim it—if anyone could push Mason back into a version of himself she understood—it was Brandy Jewel.

Evelyn lifted her glass and smiled, resolve settling quietly beneath the surface. She wasn't ready to let go. Not yet. Brandy gave some options. Then Evelyn shook her head. "You're right. I want to do this right."

Brandy studied Evelyn. "You still care."

Evelyn met her gaze. "Enough to know when I've lost."

"Leave it to me dear, you haven't lost until I say you have."

They spoke for a while longer—about Mason's stubborn streak, Jasmine's boldness, how quickly curiosity could turn into attachment. Brandy listened, filing away every observation. Then her phone buzzed. She glanced at the screen and rose. "Excuse me." Brandy stepped away, answering quietly. "Yes?"

"We're making progress," the PI said. "You shouldn't have any trouble removing her."

Brandy stilled. "Explain."

"I need a few more days to firm everything up, but her father? Major con man. Long history. Multiple aliases. Slippery."

A slow, satisfied smile curved Brandy's lips. "Lovely." she said coolly. "Get me what I asked for?"

"You don't want details now?"

"I'm at dinner," Brandy replied. "Yes or no will suffice."

"Yes."

"Good." She ended the call. When Brandy returned to the table, her expression was composed.

"Everything alright?" Evelyn asked.

"Perfectly," Brandy said. "Just business." They finished their meal without returning to the topic. When it was time to leave, Brandy stood and smoothed her jacket. "Thank you for your time, Evelyn," she said warmly. "You've been very helpful."

Evelyn hesitated. "Will you let me know?"

Brandy smiled—a thin, decisive curve of her lips. "Of course. I'll be in touch once Jasmine is history."

Evelyn watched her go, unease settling in her chest. Brandy stepped into the night, unbothered. This was still Jewel business. And Jasmine Franklin—she simply hadn't made the cut.

* * *

Jasmine was at home when there was a knock at her door. Looking through the peephole, she saw two gentlemen dressed in suits, and they identified themselves as detectives. They were polite, measured, their voices carefully neutral. They asked if they could come inside, just for a moment. The world seemed to narrow as soon as she saw their badges, a familiar dread settling into her chest.

They told her that her father was dead. Murdered.

The words landed without sound, like snow falling into deep water. Jasmine didn't cry. She didn't scream. Her hands trembled, but she clasped them together, grounding herself in the present. She felt sick, happy, sad, and so many other emotions. They asked questions—when she'd last seen him, when she'd last spoken to him, whether she knew anyone who might want to hurt him.

She answered them all. Yes, she had seen him recently. No, they weren't close. She explained his past without excuses, without embellishment. She told them about the cons, the lies, the way he drifted in and out of her life like a storm she could never outrun. She made it clear that while they shared blood, they didn't share a relationship.

The officers thanked her, their expressions softening with something like sympathy. When they left, Jasmine stood very still, grief pressing in not as sharp pain but as a dull, exhausting weight. Numb.

Jack had been a terrible father. A terrible person. A con man with a smile too easy and a conscience too flexible. She knew that. She'd always known that. But still, their time together hadn't always been bad. When Jack scored big, he always came home to her. He'd sweep in—loud, confident, full of stories—and take her out to eat like they were celebrating something important. He bought useless things she didn't want or need, trinkets meant to stand in for time he hadn't given. It never worked, but she'd learned to accept the gesture for what it was: love, Jack-style.

A memory rose unbidden. She had been thirteen. Jack had been gone nearly three weeks—long enough that her teacher started asking questions. Jasmine rode the bus every morning, kept the house clean, washed her clothes carefully so no one would notice the absence. Jack always left money. Food money. Emergency money. Even then, she understood the rules: stay quiet, stay smart, stay invisible.

She'd been good at that. Too good. Mrs. Batty hadn't liked it. Her teacher's smile had been too tight, her eyes too curious. *"I really need to speak with your father, Jasmine."* Jasmine had explained—politely, repeatedly—that he was busy. That messages could be left with her. That she'd pass them along.

Mrs. Batty insisted. Phone calls were made. Messages were left on their home phone. Then another—requesting an in-person conference when no one called back. Jasmine had signed Jack's name perfectly on her report card, all A's and B's, neat and proud like that should have been enough. It wasn't.

So she'd left Jack a voicemail on the cell phone number no one else knew he had. Calm. Clear. The date. The time. What the teacher wanted. She'd gone to school that day with dread sitting heavy in her stomach, rehearsing excuses, preparing to smile and apologize for a father she couldn't control.

And then she'd walked into the classroom afterschool and seen him. Jack—leaning casually against a desk, laughing with Mrs. Batty like he belonged there. Like he hadn't been gone at all.

He'd spotted her instantly. Grinned. Gestured her over. "Turns out," he'd said, "your teacher's been trying to reach me because she thinks you should be enrolled in advanced classes." Jasmine had stared at him, stunned. "I told her," Jack continued, glancing at Mrs. Batty, "That it's Jasmine's call. She's already doing great, and I don't want to put any undue pressure on her."

Mrs. Batty had beamed. "I completely agree."

Jasmine hadn't needed time to think. "I'm good where I am," she'd said quickly.

Mrs. Batty pressed. "Are you sure? It'll look great on your transcripts for college."

"Positive, I don't want to do it."

Jack had made a whole show of standing. "Well, there you have it. Jasmine wants to stay put."

He'd charmed Mrs. Batty a little longer, apologized for being hard to reach—*"Work keeps me busy, but Jasmine always makes sure I get the important messages."* Mrs. Batty had nodded sympathetically, promising not to bother him unless absolutely necessary.

As soon as they'd stepped outside, Jack had turned to her and smiled. "Thanks for the call, Jas. I always got your back." Then he'd slung an arm around her shoulders. "Now let's go get some dinner while I tell you about this schmuck I steamrolled in Atlanta." That was

Jack. Impulsive. Over-the-top. Irresponsible. But underneath it all—somewhere deep and buried—he cared.

Jasmine blinked back to the present, breath catching. Jack was gone. She'd wanted freedom for so long. Freedom from his chaos, his danger, his constant pull toward trouble. She had it now. No more cons. No more looking over her shoulder. No more bargaining pieces of her life away.

She was free. And she was alone. Jack and Susan had been their parents only children. There were no distant cousins, no grandparents. Just her. The numbness cracked just enough for grief to slip through. Not for the man he was—but for the father he sometimes tried to be.

Jasmine stared at her phone for a long moment before pressing Mason's name. Her thumb hovered, then she exhaled and hit call.

"Hey," Mason answered, warmth immediate.

"Hi."

"Everything okay?"

"Can you come over?" Her voice was steady, almost too steady. "I could use your company tonight."

There was a pause, just long enough for him to hear something was wrong. "Yeah. Of course. I'll be there."

When he arrived, she let him in without a word and led him to the couch. She sat beside him, close but not touching at first, her hands folded in her lap as if she were bracing herself.

"My dad died today," she said.

Mason blinked, the words taking a second to register. He turned toward her, searching her face for tears that weren't there. "Jasmine … I'm so sorry." She nodded once. Just a quiet acceptance that felt heavier than any breakdown. Mason hesitated, unsure what she needed, then gently rested his hand over hers. "Is there anything I can do?"

She looked at him then, her eyes sad. She swallowed. "He wasn't a good father, Mason. He was barely a father at all." He waited, giving her space to continue, but she didn't. "That's all I want to say about it," she added, almost apologetically. "Please don't ask questions. Not tonight."

"Okay," he said immediately. No pressure. No curiosity edging into his voice. Just understanding.

She finally leaned into him, resting her head against his shoulder like it was the most natural place in the world. "I don't need advice. I don't need fixing. I just... need you here."

Mason wrapped his arm around her without hesitation, holding her gently but firmly, as if anchoring her in place. "I'm not going anywhere."

Jasmine closed her eyes, breathing him in. For the first time that day, the ache in her chest eased—not because the pain was gone, but because she didn't have to carry it alone. They stayed like that for a while, the world muted around them. Eventually, Mason pressed a kiss to the top of her head and shifted just enough to look at her.

"Have you eaten?" he asked softly.

She shook her head. "Didn't think about it."

"Okay," he said, already reaching for his phone. "I've got this."

She watched him scroll, brow furrowed in concentration, and despite everything, a small smile tugged at her lips. "You know, you could cook."

Mason barked out a laugh. "Absolutely not."

"Oh, come on."

"I'm a danger to myself and others in a kitchen," he said solemnly. "That's why I employ professionals."

She grabbed a pillow and swatted him lightly. "Must be nice."

"It's survival," he replied, grinning.

He ordered food—comfort food, not flashy—checking with her on everything. When it arrived, they ate on the couch, knees touching, trading stories that skirted around grief without denying it. He told her about the time he tried to make pasta in college and nearly set off the fire alarm. She laughed for the first time all day, the sound soft but real.

"That was my cue to invest in restaurants instead," he said. "Much safer."

They flipped on the TV, some mindless comedy playing in the background. Jasmine leaned into him, her head resting against his chest. Mason's arm tightened instinctively, thumb tracing slow, grounding circles against her shoulder.

At some point, her breathing evened out. She'd fallen asleep. Mason smiled down at her, careful not to move too suddenly. He watched her for a moment—lashes resting against her cheeks, face relaxed in sleep—and something deep in his chest settled into place. He gently lifted her, surprised again by how natural it felt, and carried her to the bedroom. She stirred just enough to murmur his name, arms curling briefly around his neck before relaxing again.

"I've got you," he whispered. He laid her down carefully and hesitated only a second before sliding into the bed beside her, pulling the covers up and tucking her close to him. She shifted toward him automatically, fitting against him like she belonged there. Mason stared at the ceiling, heart steady, certain.

It wasn't the right moment to say it. She was grieving, raw, and he wouldn't add weight to a night already heavy with emotion. But the truth was there, clear and undeniable. This—being here, holding her, choosing her in the quiet moments—this felt right. And when the time came, he'd find exactly the right time to tell her he loved her.

* * *

Brandy didn't waste time.

She requested to meet Jasmine, her tone almost kind as her assistant poured tea neither of them would touch. Jasmine sensed the trap before it closed, her shoulders tense as Brandy folded her hands neatly on the table. Jasmine didn't want to be there, but this was Mason's mother after all.

Brandy didn't bother with small talk. "I'm not going to pretend this is a social visit," she said calmly. "I don't have the patience for that, and I don't think you do either."

Jasmine met her gaze. "Then say what you brought me here to say."

Brandy's lips tightened, almost into an approving smile. "I know about you and your father." Jasmine didn't flinch, but her insides froze with panic. "I know about the con games. The arrests. The aliases. The trail he left behind." She tilted her head slightly. "I also know he's dead."

Her heart clenched at that last part, he'd only been gone for a few weeks now but it still didn't seem real.

Jasmine's fingers curled in fists under the table. "Congratulations. You did your homework."

Brandy ignored the edge in her voice. "What interests me is how convenient it all looks. A charming con man's daughter. A well-practiced smile. My son, the gullible rich lover." She paused, letting the implication settle. "Mason trusts too easily. He always has. He loves deeply. Completely. And that makes him vulnerable. As his mother, I have to make sure I protect him and our assets."

Jasmine's jaw tightened. "I'm not my father."

"That's not how stories work, dear," Brandy replied evenly. "They don't need to be true. They just need to be believable. And with the right framing, yours is."

Silence stretched between them.

"You will walk away," Brandy said at last. "Spare Mason any confusion. Any suspicion. Or"—her eyes sharpened—"I could tell him what I know about you. About your father. About what his involvement with you may have cost him."

Jasmine stood abruptly, the chair scraping softly against the floor. "You don't get to rewrite my life. This isn't some Lifetime movie; you can't be this crazy."

Brandy rose too, unbothered. "I get to protect my son. Getting rid of you is a bonus."

Jasmine laughed once, short and hollow. "You're not protecting him, you're protecting your 'assets.'"

Brandy didn't answer. She didn't have to. Inside, Jasmine was splitting in two. One part of her wanted to turn around—to plant her feet, lift her chin, and fight. Mason had become more than a relationship. He was safety. Choice. Her love. A future she hadn't even realized she was allowing herself to imagine until it was suddenly at risk. The thought of losing him made her chest tighten, her breath shallow, like she was already drowning. The other part of her—the part shaped by years of survival—knew exactly how this ended.

"You know what's funny?" Jasmine said, keeping her voice steady even as her thoughts raced. "For someone who says she's protecting her son, you never once thought about his happiness in this."

Brandy didn't flinch. "Happiness is temporary; he will have another one of you in no time."

Jasmine swallowed. She could already see it playing out. Mason finding out about her past not from her—but from Brandy. About Jack. About the cons. About the things Jasmine had done to survive, to keep the peace, to finally earn her freedom. Information delivered strategically, surgically—just enough truth twisted into something ugly.

He'd believe Brandy. Or worse, he'd doubt Jasmine. And doubt would be enough to change the way he looked at her. Jasmine looked away first, her voice softer when she spoke again. "He'd believe you. Or at least… he'd question me. And that would be enough."

Brandy studied her, cool and assessing. "Then you understand the position you're in."

Jasmine nodded slowly, the weight of it pressing down on her chest. "Yes. I do."

She should have seen this coming. Mason had warned her—told her his mother didn't back down; she escalated. And man, he'd been right. Jasmine's fingers curled around the strap of her bag. She thought of the night Mason held her while she mourned Jack. How she'd almost told him everything then. How that would have been the moment—the honest, raw moment—to lay it all out. But she hadn't, because she was afraid.

Afraid he'd look at her differently. Afraid that being with her would suddenly feel complicated once he knew she'd helped her father, even if she'd hated every second of it. Afraid that Jack's shadow would stretch far enough to touch Mason. Helping Jack had always carried consequences. She'd known that. She just hadn't realized the bill would come due now.

She turned back to the door. "You win, I'll call him tonight and break things off." Then she left. Outside, Jasmine leaned against the wall, breath trembling as everything she'd been holding back rushed in. Her phone felt heavy in her hand.

It was about accountability. She would end things—not to punish him, not to protect Brandy—but because she had lied through omission, and Mason Jewel deserved the truth from her lips, not his mother's weaponized version of it. The hardest part wasn't walking away. It was knowing she might be doing the right thing—and still lose him anyway.

In her car she rested her head on the seat.

Instead of calling Mason, Jasmine called Kiera. She could barely get the words out—*"Can you come over?"* Her tongue felt swollen in her mouth. That was all it took.

"I'm on my way," Kiera said immediately, already grabbing her keys.

When Kiera stepped through the door less than twenty minutes later, Jasmine didn't even try to explain. She crossed the room and collapsed into Kiera's arms, the breath she'd been holding all day finally leaving her in a shaky sigh.

"Well," Kiera said softly, wrapping her up tight, "this can't be good. What's wrong?"

Jasmine pulled back just enough to look at her. "I met with Brandy."

Kiera froze. "Oh."

"Yeah," Jasmine whispered. "*Oh.*"

They sat on the couch; Jasmine curled in on herself while Kiera listened. Jasmine told her everything—about Brandy's calm cruelty, about the unspoken threat, about realizing Mason would hear her past from someone else if she didn't act first.

"Oh honey, and while your still grieving Jack you have to deal with this."

"I told her she won," Jasmine said, staring at her hands. "That I'd end things with Mason."

Kiera's mouth fell open. "Jas—"

"I was mad," Jasmine continued, her voice thick. "And sad. And terrified. I didn't know what else to do."

Kiera shifted closer. "Okay. First of all, breathe. Second—are you *sure* Mason would even care?"

Jasmine let out a bitter laugh. "Yes. And not because he's judgmental. He hates lying and manipulation. He grew up drowning in it. Finding out I kept something this big from him?" She shook her head. "I couldn't stand it if he looked at me like that."

"You didn't lie," Kiera said. "You just ... haven't told him yet."

"I lied by omission," Jasmine said firmly. "And I had the perfect moment to tell him—when Jack died. I didn't because I was scared."

Kiera sighed. "You're both clearly in love. Give him the chance to decide for himself."

"I can't," Jasmine said. "Not when it'll look like I'm coming clean just to get ahead of Brandy. I don't want him thinking I'm a con woman or a gold digger."

Kiera reached out, lifting Jasmine's chin. Her big brown eyes—warm, expressive, full of compassion—held Jasmine steady. "You are neither of those things. And if Mason doesn't see that, then that's on him."

They talked for a long while, circling the same fears, the same impossible choices. Kiera kept pushing for honesty. Jasmine kept pulling back, wanting to disappear quietly instead of detonating everything.

Eventually, Kiera glanced at the clock and groaned. "I need to run home and grab some papers I need for this signing tomorrow and I will stay the night."

Jasmine sat up straighter. "You should go. I'm okay now."

"No."

"Yes," Jasmine insisted softly. "I still have to call Mason. And once I'm done, I'm going to lie in bed and eat ice cream."

Kiera blinked. "I can eat ice cream in bed with you."

Jasmine smiled faintly for the first time all night. "You can—but I'm going to want to be alone." She stood and pulled Kiera into another hug, holding on longer this time. "Go. I'll call you tomorrow with the details of this train wreck I call my life."

Kiera hugged her back fiercely. "You don't call me; I'm coming over. I'll use my emergency key. I won't knock."

Jasmine laughed weakly. "Noted."

They hugged again, reluctant, before Kiera finally left. When the door closed, the house felt too quiet. Jasmine sank back onto the couch, phone heavy in her hand, heart pounding. Ice cream could wait. She stared at Mason's name on her screen, swallowed hard, and braced herself for the hardest call she'd ever have to make.

The way he looked at her like she was something rare. The way he listened. The way she'd almost let herself believe that her past didn't matter anymore.

She believed Mason would want to trust her. But she also knew how doubt worked—how easily it crept in when planted by someone who claimed to be protecting him, and there was just enough truth that the lie would be indistinguishable. She knew he wouldn't choose his mother over her. She knew their history; Mason didn't trust his mother any more than she did. Brandy had just enough to make him question if Jasmine would be truthful. Jasmine would have to tell him about the things she'd done, things she wasn't proud of.

So, she made the only choice that felt like love.

Breaking things off would hurt him and her, but staying could destroy her in ways she couldn't predict or control. She wouldn't give Brandy the satisfaction of a public accusation or a whispered scandal. She would simply step away, carrying the pain herself. As she reached for her phone, Jasmine whispered a quiet goodbye—to the future she'd almost had, and to the hope that one day, Mason might understand why she walked away.

* * *

Brandy smiled at the closed door, sat down and leaned back in her chair, a slow, satisfied smirk curving her lips.

Silly girl. She really thought she would win this war.

Brandy reached for her desk phone and pressed a button. "Get me Mason's schedule for the next couple of weeks. I need to know if he's going out of town and what social events he's attending."

There was a pause on the other end. "Ms. Jewel, you know he will not share that information with me," her assistant said carefully.

Brandy's smile vanished. "Then find a way to get it," she snapped. "Don't you assistants talk?"

A nervous beat. "No worries, Ms. Jewel. I'll get it."

"See that you do." Brandy hung up without another word.

She didn't waste time. Her fingers moved to her cell phone, scrolling until she found the number she wanted.

Evelyn.

The call connected, and Brandy didn't bother with pleasantries. "I got his little girlfriend out of the way. He'll be sad—and prime for your advances."

Evelyn's breath hitched. "Are you serious?"

"Very," Brandy said coolly. "I'll text you a list of places you can conveniently 'bump into' him at. With Jasmine out of the way he should be in a better head space to listen to an old familiar 'friend'. The rest is up to you."

On the other end, Evelyn practically vibrated with excitement. "I'll cancel my appointments. Emergency hair, wax, new dresses—whatever it takes. I can make him forget all about her. No problem."

Brandy allowed herself a thin smile. "See that you do. And don't mess it up this time. Because this will be your last opportunity."

The message was clear.

Evelyn swallowed, hearing the threat beneath the words. "You won't be disappointed."

"Good," Brandy said. "You won't get another chance."

She ended the call and stared out the window, the city lights reflecting in her eyes.

Mason thought he was in control.

Jasmine thought she was safe.

Brandy Jewel knew better.

CHAPTER 7

Mason was reading through a proposal when his phone rang. Jasmine's name lit up the screen, and for a split second, relief washed over him. Things had felt off tonight—quiet, distant. She'd called off dinner and hadn't returned any of his texts.

"Hey."

"Hey." Her voice was soft, almost distracted.

He put down his papers, giving her his full attention. "What's going on?"

There was a pause, the faint sound of her breathing on the line. "I don't think this is working, Mason."

If he wasn't sure they were on the phone, he would have sworn she'd slapped him. He leaned back against his chair, gripping the arm. "What do you mean? What exactly isn't working?"

"I've been thinking about us," she said carefully. "I think I need some space. I think we're just ... from different worlds. Different lives. Sometimes that kind of difference catches up to people."

"That's what this is?" His jaw tightened. "Different worlds?"

"Yes."

"That's not a reason. That's something people say when they don't want to tell the truth." Silence stretched. He could almost picture her, eyes down, choosing restraint over honesty.

"I'm not trying to hurt you," she said finally. "I just don't see this working long-term."

Mason exhaled sharply. "You don't *see* it, or you don't want to try?"

"It's better to stop now, before it gets harder."

A bitter laugh escaped him. "This feels less hard to you?" He ran a hand down his face, anger flaring beneath the hurt. "You know what? I fell in love with you." Her breath caught—just barely—but she didn't interrupt. "I fell in love with your beauty," he continued hoping this would make her understand what she meant to him, voice steady despite the ache in his chest. "With how smart you are. With the fact that you don't pretend. You're honest, unfiltered. That was easy. Loving you is easy."

Silence.

"I think you believe that now, but it won't always be that way."

"Why all this doubt about us now? We've been so good together. The way you moaned my name last night was real. But in todays light I don't think your good enough?"

She said his name, quiet and pleading, but he kept going.

"What wouldn't be easy," he said, lowering his voice, "is spending my life reassuring you that you're enough. Or convincing you I'm not secretly looking for something more. I won't live like that." The line was silent. "So if you've already decided this won't work," he went on, swallowing hard, "then maybe it's for the best you're ending it. Because I deserve to be with someone who believes I'd choose them."

"I'm sorry," Jasmine said, her voice breaking just enough to hurt.

Mason closed his eyes and sighed. "Yeah. Me too."

He ended the call before either of them could say something they couldn't take back. The office felt too small afterward, papers forgotten. Mason stood there for a long moment, anger and grief tangled together, but beneath it all was clarity. He wouldn't chase someone who had already decided to leave. And as much as it hurt, he knew letting her go was the only way to keep his dignity intact.

* * *

Jasmine didn't realize she was crying until the tears dropped onto her hand.

The call had ended, the screen had gone dark, and she'd sat there staring at her phone like it might light up again if she waited long enough. Then the first tear fell. Then another. And suddenly she was crying—really crying—the kind that shook her shoulders and stole the air from her lungs.

And then, through the tears, she laughed. It startled her, the sound rough and unfamiliar. She pressed a hand over her mouth, shaking her head. She couldn't remember the last time she'd cried like this. Not when her father disappeared for months at a time. Not when she learned to stop expecting anyone to stay. And now here she was, undone over a breakup.

"Of course," she whispered hoarsely. "Of course it's this."

She let the tears come, no longer fighting them. Mason would walk away believing this was about her doubts, her insecurities, some quiet fear that she wasn't enough. That lie was almost merciful. The truth was far worse, heavier than anything she could ever put into words without destroying him in the process.

Brandy. The threat. The twisted story waiting to be told. Would stay that way now that Jasmine was out of the picture.

He thought she'd left because she didn't trust his love. The thought made her cry harder. His words replayed in her head, uninvited and relentless. *"I fell in love with you."* She folded forward, pressing her forehead to her knees as a sob tore out of her. She hadn't even let herself think the word. Love felt dangerous—too big, too hopeful, too easy to weaponize. She'd locked it away, told herself she was being careful.

But it was already too late. She loved him. Loved the way he listened without trying to fix her. Loved how safe she felt in his presence. Loved how easily he chose her. Loved the way he loved her body. And the cruelest part of all was knowing he loved her too—openly, without hesitation—while she was the one walking away.

When the tears finally slowed, Jasmine reached for her phone again with shaking hands and tapped Kiera's name. She should of asked her to stay.

She answered on the second ring. "Hey."

"I'm going to get some ice cream, I just needed a friendly voice first." Jasmine broke all over again. "I did it."

There was no judgment on the other end. No sharp intake of breath. Just a soft, steady, "Oh, Jassy."

"I broke up with him," Jasmine said, her voice cracking. "I didn't tell him. I couldn't. He thinks it's me. He thinks it's my fear of his money."

Kiera sighed gently. "I told you not to do it like this."

Jasmine huffed out a weak, tearful laugh. "Yeah. Great advice from someone not living my life."

"I know," Kiera said immediately. "And I'm not saying I told you so. I'm just here."

That was why she called. Kiera knew everything—her father, Brandy, the threat. All of it. They'd been friends since high school, since before Jasmine learned how to hide the messier parts of herself. Kiera didn't sugarcoat, but she never judged.

"I love him," Jasmine whispered.

"I know," Kiera said softly.

"I ruined it anyway."

"No," Kiera replied. "You protected him. Even if it hurts like hell."

Jasmine closed her eyes, fresh tears slipping free. "Tell me it's going to be okay."

There was a pause—just a breath too long to be comforting. "I won't lie to you," Kiera said gently. "It's going to hurt. For a while. Maybe a long while. But you're not broken. And you're not alone."

Jasmine nodded even though Kiera couldn't see her. She curled into herself, phone pressed to her ear, letting the quiet truth settle in.

It wasn't okay, but her best friend was still there. And for now, that would have to be enough.

* * *

Mason had been a bear this week. This was the worst time for the board to be meeting on a new campaign. His patience ran thin; his answers were clipped. He snapped at nothing, brooded over everything, and by dinner, he'd pushed his plate away untouched, barking at everyone to finish so he could leave.

"Geez," Tiffany said once he'd left the room, "I'm glad this was our last meeting for a month. I don't know what's up his butt."

Brandy's lips curved with satisfaction as she sipped her wine. "Grumpy, yes. But he'll recover. He's better off now."

Tiffany frowned. "Better off from what?"

Brandy set her glass down, clearly pleased to elaborate. "From that woman. Jasmine. I told you she was trouble and now they're broken up."

Tiffany smirked. "Nothing gets past you. How do you know they broke up?"

"Because I made it happen." She was bored with this conversation already. "She was trouble so I made it go away."

Tiffany straightened. "What kind of trouble?"

"A con woman," Brandy said smoothly. "Or at the very least, well trained by one. Her father made a career out of scamming people, and she learned at his knee. Gold digging, manipulation—Mason never stood a chance."

Tiffany stared at her mother. "You're serious."

"Completely," Brandy replied. "I did what I had to do to protect my son."

Something cold settled in Tiffany's stomach. "What does that mean?"

Brandy waved a dismissive hand. "I hired a private investigator. I needed facts before things went any further. And what I found confirmed everything."

"You hired a PI," Tiffany repeated slowly. "On Mason's girlfriend."

"Ex-girlfriend. And yes. Any good mother would."

Tiffany forced her expression to smooth out, schooling her face into something close to approval. "Wow. That's ... thorough."

Brandy smiled, mistaking restraint for agreement. "You'll understand when you have children."

Tiffany excused herself a few minutes later, her jaw tight, fury buzzing just under her skin. Their mother wasn't protective. She was manipulative. And Mason was collateral damage.

Tiffany sat alone in her office, hands clenched on the edge of her desk.

Their mother was so manipulative it was almost impressive—if it weren't so exhausting. Some days, Tiffany had to fight the absurd impulse to check whether Brandy had been quietly replaced by a Disney villain. The calm smile. The absolute certainty that she was always right. The way she framed control as love.

Tiffany couldn't remember a time when her mother hadn't been controlling. From the time she was young, Tiffany had tried to be exactly what Brandy wanted—poised, brilliant, beautiful, powerful. She had become all of those things. And it still wasn't enough. She showed up early. Stayed late. Hit every metric. Every goal. *Do this. Date him. Smile more. Be strategic.*

It never changed. If Tiffany were honest with herself, she couldn't wait to be out from under her mother's shadow. Making Brandy happy had once been her highest goal, the thing she oriented her entire life around. But somewhere along the way, that shifted.

She still wanted the money. Still wanted the power. She loved being the CFO of one of the largest pharmaceutical companies in the world—and she fully intended to be CEO one day. But she also knew the truth: that promotion wouldn't happen until her mother was dead and gone. Brandy wasn't leaving that seat without a fight.

And lately, that didn't bother her. Tiffany wanted more. More ease.

More space to breathe. A man who understood her without seeing her as a stepping stone or an accessory. Someone who appreciated her, not just her resumé. Maybe even children. The thought used to horrify her—spit-up on Chanel, sticky fingers near priceless furniture. Now? It didn't make her want to cry anymore.

She was changing. And the biggest shift of all was this: she no longer believed her mother was always right. She just didn't argue anymore. Arguing was pointless. Brandy didn't listen—she conquered. So Tiffany had learned to go around her instead. Smile. Nod. Pretend they were aligned while quietly doing exactly what she wanted behind the scenes.

Mason had never played that game. He and their mother butted heads like it was their purpose in life. Mason had always been his own man, stubborn and principled, and he reminded Tiffany so much of their father it sometimes hurt. He had their father's good looks, good heart, his integrity—and the same no-nonsense edge when pushed too far.

They weren't the closest siblings. They'd lived parallel lives more often than shared ones. Mason didn't approve of the way Tiffany navigated power or how easily she bent to their mother's will. But when it counted—when things truly mattered—he was there. No questions. No conditions.

Tiffany didn't like his do-gooder attitude. So what if she liked dating rich men? She didn't see him dating the ladies at your local fast food joint. He made it his business to volunteer and give back or whatever. Tiffany wrote checks, which did the same good in her book.

She wasn't a manual-labor type of girl—and she didn't pretend to be. They had different views on life, different ways of moving through the world.

But he was still her little brother.

And no matter what, she would protect him whenever and however she could.

That loyalty went both ways. Which was why Tiffany couldn't let this go. Their mother had crossed a line. Again. Hiring a private investigator. Digging into a woman Mason cared about. Manipulating circumstances until she forced Jasmine out of the picture and then calling it "protection."

If Jasmine was a gold digger, that was Mason's lesson to learn—not Brandy's mess to engineer. Mason deserved the dignity of his own mistakes. And if Jasmine wasn't what their mother claimed... Tiffany's jaw tightened. Then Brandy had destroyed something real for no reason other than control.

She reached for her phone, staring at Mason's name for a long moment before locking the screen again. Not yet. But soon. Because for the first time in a long while, Tiffany knew exactly where she stood. And it wasn't on her mother's side.

* * *

Tiffany went to his home later that night. Mason was sitting in the dark with only the TV on for background noise.

"Didn't I ask you to stop using that key? It's for emergencies only." Without looking up from the TV.

"You look like hell," Tiffany said gently.

"Funny. I feel worse."

She sat across from him, leaning forward. "I need to tell you something. And you're not going to like it."

He looked at her then, something wary flickering in his eyes. "That bad?"

"Yeah," she said. "It is."

She didn't ease into it. She told him everything—about Brandy hiring a private investigator, about the file, about how their mother had painted Jasmine as a gold digger and a con artist trained by her father. She told him how casually Brandy had said it, how pleased she'd been with herself.

Mason went very still. "This is insane even for her."

"She interfered," Tiffany said. "Big time. And I don't know exactly what she said to Jasmine—or threatened—but I know Mother. She doesn't bluff when she thinks she's right."

His hands clenched slowly. "Why is she like this?"

Tiffany snorted. "A Bond villain? No idea, but it wasn't Grammy's fault; she was a delight." Tiffany's attempt at humor fell short. Silence stretched, thick and heavy. "I don't know if Jasmine did anything wrong," Tiffany continued carefully. "But I do know this: you can't trust Mother's version of the story. Not when she's decided someone is the enemy."

Mason swallowed, pain and anger flashing across his face. "Jasmine never asked me for anything. Not money. Not favors. Nothing."

"That doesn't matter to her and you know it," Tiffany said softly. "That's why I'm telling you. Don't take my word for it. Don't take Mother's either. Check it out yourself. Get the facts. *You* decide. Not Mother."

He leaned back, rubbing a hand over his face. "She broke up with me out of nowhere."

"Yeah," Tiffany said. "That sounds like Mother's doing, too."

Mason looked at his sister, something like gratitude breaking through the hurt. "Why are you telling me this?"

"Because you're my brother," she said simply. "And because Mother was way out of line."

She stood, heading for the door, then paused. "Whatever you decide to do next, just make sure it's *your* decision. Not hers. I was never here, and you didn't hear any of this from me. Got it?"

"Got it." He agreed, knowing how their mother viewed betrayal. "I won't say a word to her as usual."

When Tiffany left, Mason sat alone in the quiet, her words echoing in his mind. For the first time since the breakup, doubt shifted—not about Jasmine, but about the story he'd been handed. And that changed everything.

* * *

It had only been a couple of weeks, but Jasmine felt like she was moving through fog. Everything reminded her of Mason—his coffee mug still in her cabinet, a spare tie draped over the back of a chair, a pair of socks shoved between her couch cushions like they had a mind of their own.

She hated how small the things were. Hated how big they felt.

She stood in her living room holding his toothbrush, staring at it like it had personally betrayed her.

"I could just send his stuff back," she said quietly. "Or call him to come get it."

Kiera, stretched out on the couch with a glass of wine, shook her head immediately. "Don't be that girl. He is not going to care about a toothbrush and some socks. He's worth Billions."

"It's more than that," Jasmine whined. "It's... symbolic."

"It's you looking for an excuse to hear his voice," Kiera corrected gently.

Jasmine sighed and dropped the toothbrush back into the cup. "You're probably right."

"If you're going to call him," Kiera continued, "do it for real. Tell him you made a mistake. Tell him Brandy threatened you and your fight-or-flight kicked in. Tell him low blood sugar made you do it if you have to."

Jasmine let out a sad laugh. "Low blood sugar is a valid villain."

Kiera grinned. "Listen, I don't know why I'm single. I'm beautiful, funny, and clearly a life coach at this point."

Jasmine smiled despite herself. "You really are."

"And other than my skin tone," Kiera added, striking a pose, "I could be Tammy from Love & Hip Hop's sister. They're threatened by this full package."

That got a real laugh out of Jasmine. A small one—but real.

Then Kiera sobered. "All jokes aside, you can fix this. Mason seems like a reasonable man. He cares about you. You don't just walk away from that because of fear."

Jasmine's smile faded.

Secrets she couldn't share.

"I didn't just leave because of fear," Jasmine said softly. "I left because I didn't want him hurt because of me."

Kiera's voice softened too. "Baby, he's already hurt because you're gone."

That hit harder than anything else.

Jasmine looked down at her phone sitting on the coffee table. His name still sat at the top of her favorites. Untouched. Uncalled.

"I miss him," she whispered.

"Then stop punishing yourself," Kiera said. "And stop letting other people control your story."

Jasmine picked up her phone, thumb hovering over Mason's name.

"No," Jasmine said quietly. "It's better this way. Let him start over with someone less complicated. There's too much there."

Kiera studied her. "I would shake some sense into you if I thought it would help. That's not what this is really about."

"I did help Jack with some of his cons," Jasmine admitted. "I'm not a bad person, but I am not innocent. People with that kind of money always question motives. I don't want Mason to ever wonder about mine. I don't want him looking at me and thinking, is she here because of me... or because of what I have?"

She swallowed.

"Besides, he's probably already moving on. As soon as it was known he was single, I bet he had to beat women away with a bat."

Kiera frowned. "No one falls out of love that fast."

Jasmine forced a small smile. "You don't know that."

"I do," Kiera said firmly. Then she added, trying to lighten it, "You can make all the excuses you want. I already forgave you for taking his billions away from us. As your best friend, I was really looking forward to the riding your coattail. Maybe even a rich best-friend hookup situation."

Jasmine snorted despite herself.

"Don't play with my heart or his," Kiera continued, her tone turning serious again. "If you can't call him and be honest, then leave him alone."

Jasmine heard the truth beneath the joke.

She nodded slowly. Kiera was right.

She missed Mason more than she wanted to admit. But she wasn't ready to tell him what his mother had done. She wasn't ready to tell him about Jack. About the parts of her past that still scared her.

So she would let him go.

She would give her heart time to heal instead of drowning it in self-pity. She would build her business, one client at a time. She would focus on the life she was creating with her own hands.

It wasn't the life she'd imagined with Mason.

But for now... it would have to be enough.

Jasmine set her phone face down on the table.

* * *

Evelyn watched Mason from across the room as he sat with two other men, laughing and eating dinner. To anyone else, he looked perfectly fine—relaxed, engaged, the picture of success.

But she knew better.

The sadness was in his eyes.

It was the same professional mask he always wore for the world. The one that said everything was fine when it wasn't.

I can make him forget her, Evelyn thought. In no time.

When Mason excused himself, Evelyn waited a beat before following. She lingered near the hallway outside the restroom, smoothing her dress and steadying her breath.

When he came out, she stepped forward.

"Fancy meeting you here, stranger."

Mason looked at her like she was a gnat. "Evelyn, good to see you." he said flatly, already moving to go around her.

"I was hoping to have a moment of your time," she said quickly, blocking his path just enough to force him to stop.

"I'm here on a business meeting," Mason replied coolly, "and I have a date right after."

He emphasized the word date.

Evelyn frowned. Brandy had assured her he wasn't seeing anyone.

"I heard you and Yasmine broke up," she said coyly. "Back on the market. Lucky us."

Mason exhaled, clearly irritated. "It's Jasmine. And yes, I'm single. But no—I'm not interested in picking up where we left off."

Her smile faltered.

"Even if you weren't my mother's lackey," he continued, his tone firm, "your complete disregard for what I wanted in that relationship is the reason we could never be together."

He stepped back. "I wish you nothing but the best."

And with that, he walked around her.

Evelyn stood frozen for a second before hot tears filled her eyes. She turned quickly and rushed into the restroom, locking herself in a stall.

A few tears slipped free before she angrily wiped them away.

She wished—just for a moment—that he wasn't a Jewel. That she could call her father and make Mason pay for making her feel this small.

Did he know who she was?

Of course he did.

And he didn't care.

Men usually fell over themselves to be with her. Rich men. Powerful men. Attractive men. Mason wasn't the only one out there.

She refused to keep embarrassing herself over a man who clearly didn't want her.

Brandy can have this circus, she thought bitterly.

Evelyn straightened her spine, left the stall, fixed her makeup, and checked her reflection.

Then she pulled out her phone and sent a text.

One of her suitors would be more than happy to fly her somewhere beautiful, spoil her properly, and show her a good time.

Resolved, she squared her shoulders and walked out.

If Mason Jewel didn't want her—

Someone else certainly would.

CHAPTER 8

Mason told everyone it was a business trip.

Technically, it was true. Meetings were scheduled. Calls were taken. He sat through presentations and nodded at the right moments. But none of it touched him. His body was present; his mind was somewhere else, circling the same conversation, the same ending, the same woman who had walked away without really leaving him. Distance hadn't dulled it. If anything, it sharpened everything.

The hotel room was too quiet when his phone finally rang. "Talk to me," Mason said the moment he saw the name on the caller ID.

"I finished the background," the PI replied. "You were right to ask for the full package and discretion."

Mason stood by the window, city lights blurring together below. He'd been waiting on this call for what felt like weeks. "And?"

A pause came, just long enough to brace him.

"Jasmine's father was murdered," the PI said. Mason closed his eyes. "Case is officially unsolved. Unofficially? It's not much of a priority from what I can tell. He had a reputation—petty crimes, scams, burned a lot of people. The kind of man police assume earned his ending."

"That doesn't make him less dead," Mason said quietly.

"No, but it made him easy to forget."

Mason's jaw tightened hating he had to ask. "Was she involved?"

"Can't say for sure, but the police don't like her for it," the PI said without hesitation. "They barely had a relationship. Long stretches of no contact. Occasional check-ins over the years, nothing substantial. He did pay for her college tuition, but no shared addresses or accounts. No suspicious behavior before or after his death. She had him cremated and didn't throw a funeral. Not that anyone would have come, this dude was hated worse than Trump."

Mason watched his reflection in the glass. Controlled. Still. The same mask he'd learned to wear young. "She didn't benefit?" he asked.

"Not a cent. No inheritance. No insurance, nothing. She cremated him on her dime."

"And her record?"

"Clean. Impressive, actually. Mother died in Jasmine's early teens, factory accident. Stable work history. No student loans. No legal trouble. Strong references. If she was working with her father, she was way better at it than him. I was able to get a look at her financials—that's going to cost you extra, by the way. She's not rolling in dough like you but she's comfortable, she has a healthy savings, a couple of Roth IRA's, and she's investing in the stock market. All in all, I saw no red flags. I'll have the report to you in five."

The call ended a minute later. Mason stayed where he was, phone heavy in his hand. Mother died young; father murdered. A woman who learned early how to survive without either of them. The pieces settled in his mind, not with shock—but with recognition.

People had spent years assuming he would turn out like his mother. Waited for it, watching for cracks. For proof that her cruelty, her manipulation, her absolute lack of conscience had somehow been genetic instead of chosen. They'd been wrong. He'd worked too hard to become someone else.

And Jasmine—quiet, guarded Jasmine—had done the same. He

pictured her choosing her words so carefully on the phone. Saying just enough to let him go without giving him a reason to fight. Carrying something alone because she believed it was safer that way. His chest tightened. She was protecting herself, but him as well. The realization hit with unsettling clarity: she hadn't left because she didn't believe in him. She'd left because she didn't believe she was allowed to stay.

Mason turned away from the window and crossed the room, energy coiling tight beneath his skin. He thought of his mother—of the damage she'd caused, the way people had tried to reduce him to her worst qualities. He had refused, and he refused this too.

He wasn't walking away from Jasmine because of her father's sins. He wasn't letting a dead man—one she barely knew—define her future or destroy what they had. If anything, it made him understand her better.

The decision settling into place with a steadiness that surprised him. This wasn't anger. It wasn't impulse. It was certainty. She didn't need saving, but she did need someone who wouldn't leave when things got complicated. And Mason had never been afraid of complicated.

Mason sat alone in the hotel room, the city humming far below his window, lights blurred by the glass and his own restless thoughts. They'd only been apart a few weeks, but it felt longer. Not in time—he could track every day with annoying precision—but in weight. In absence. This didn't feel like a breakup. It felt like something had been taken from him.

He hated that distinction most of all. Jasmine hadn't stormed out. She hadn't accused him, hadn't demanded anything unreasonable. She'd simply stepped away, pride and fear wrapped so tightly together he hadn't known how to separate them in the moment. At the time, he'd told himself it was stubbornness. That she was letting insecurity win. Now he knew better.

Most people saw his money as leverage. Opportunity. Security.

Jasmine had seen it as a risk. Another reason someone might decide she wasn't worth staying for. He dragged a hand down his face and exhaled slowly.

He'd tried to move on. Tried the way he always had before—quickly, decisively, without reflection. The first date had seemed harmless enough. The woman was beautiful, polished, and confident. On paper, she made sense. She even looked a little like Jasmine—same elegant bone structure, same easy smile. For a brief, foolish moment, he'd thought that might help.

It hadn't. By the time the appetizers arrived, he was already irritated. Everything the woman said reminded him of who she wasn't. Her laugh didn't land the same way. Her questions felt transactional. When she talked about her job, her goals, her connections, all Mason could think was how Jasmine used to light up talking about building something that was *hers*. He'd faked a business call and left before dessert.

The second attempt had been worse. That one had been pure impulse. A desperate, old reflex. *Get her out of your head. Sex always works.* The woman had been stunning. Shorter than his usual preference, but her face was striking, her body undeniable. She'd clocked him immediately—recognized the look, the access, the ease. She'd leaned in close at the bar, voice low, smile promising exactly what she thought he wanted. And Mason had known within seconds he was in trouble. Not because he wanted her, but because he didn't.

Every familiar signal—every invitation—only made him feel hollow. The longer she sat there, the more trapped he felt, like he was betraying something sacred by even pretending. He'd finished his drink, made a polite excuse, and left with his chest tight and his patience gone.

The next night had been when Tiffany showed up. The night before everything snapped into focus. Now he knew the truth, the whole ugly truth about his mother's interference, and the anger still lived just under his skin. If he hadn't promised Tiffany he'd hold his tongue, he would've torn into Brandy until neither of them had a voice left.

But rage wasn't what mattered, clarity was. And the clearest thing he'd realized was this: he didn't want to get over Jasmine. He loved her. Not the idea of her. Not the challenge. Not the novelty of someone unimpressed by his last name. *Her*.

Her honesty. Her restraint. The way she held her ground without hardening. The way she saw his world clearly and still chose her own. Going back to his old habits wasn't going to erase that. It wasn't going to dull it or replace it or distract him into something easier. It was just going to make him lonelier.

He would finish this business trip. He would handle what needed to be handled. And then—when his plane touched down—he knew exactly where he was going. This time, he wasn't letting her walk away without a fight. Mason picked up his phone, scrolled to Tank's name, and hit dial. Tank picked up on the second ring.

"Tell me you're calling to talk about poker," Tank said, already skeptical.

Mason let out a sharp breath. "My mother hired a private investigator. On Jasmine."

There was a beat of silence, then: "Damn," Tank said, followed by a long, low whistle. "I hate to say I was right, but … that's next-level unhinged. I knew Brandy was controlling, but this? She needs therapy. Like, professionally. With homework."

Mason huffed a humorless laugh. "It gets worse. The PI found out things about Jasmine's father. And my mother was ready to use it. Or make something up if she had to."

"Wow," Tank said slowly. "That's … evil, Mason. There's no other word for it."

"I know."

"So what are you going to do?" Tank asked.

"I'm going to talk to Jasmine," Mason said without hesitation. "I need to understand why she didn't come to me. Why she thought walking away was the only option."

Tank didn't hesitate. "Brandy," he said flatly. "That's the answer. Hell, I'd walk away too if I thought your mother was about to scorch-earth my life. Hiring a PI, threatening fake dirt? That's villain behavior."

Mason rubbed his jaw. "Yeah. I get it now. At the time, I thought it was pride or fear. But knowing what she was dealing with ... I don't blame her."

"Good," Tank said. "Because blaming her would be stupid."

Mason snorted. "You always have a way with words."

"Someone has to. So—getting back together? You have been an ass lately."

"I want to," Mason said. "I just don't know if she'll let me. Or if she'll trust that I can actually keep my mother out of it."

"That's the real problem," Tank said. "Brandy doesn't respect boundaries. She respects power. So you're going to have to make it very clear where the line is—and what happens if she crosses it."

Mason's expression hardened. "I've never let her dictate my life and I won't start now. She's about to find out her access just got cut."

Tank hummed approvingly. "There it is. Jewel backbone."

They talked through it—strategies, boundaries, contingencies. Mason cutting off information. Public unity. Consequences instead of warnings. Tank didn't sugarcoat any of it, and Mason appreciated that.

Eventually the conversation drifted, as it always did. "How's the restaurants?" Mason asked.

Tank chuckled. "Busy. Always busy. And there's this woman who keeps coming in. Sits at the bar. Orders the same thing. Pretends she's there for the food."

Mason smirked. "And she's definitely there for you. You love this, that's why your kitchen is open and people can see you cook."

"Oh, absolutely," Tank said. "Not subtle about it either. But I'm waiting for her to make the first move; she seems like she spooks easy."

Mason could picture him—built like his nickname, even back in college. Broad shoulders, thick arms, the kind of physique that looked like it had been carved, not trained. Tattoos snaked down his arms, much to his father's eternal disappointment. Brown skin with deep brown eyes. A crooked nose from an old fight. Strong jaw that made women linger longer than necessary. He made sure he was seen nightly in his restaurants, which ever one he was cooking at.

Mason shook his head. "I guarantee she's not the only one. Better watch your step."

"Probably not," Tank said. "But I like watching this one; she's keeping me interested and entertained."

"Menace," Mason said fondly.

They talked a little longer—about business, about life, about nothing that mattered and everything that did. Before hanging up, Tank added, "Poker night soon. No excuses."

"Soon. I'll bring the good whiskey."

"Damn right."

When the call ended, Mason stared out the window again, the city no longer feeling so heavy. He had a plan. And this time, he wasn't walking away.

* * *

Mason didn't announce himself. He stood on Jasmine's porch longer than he meant to, staring at the door like it might decide something for him if he waited long enough. The light inside was on. That mattered. It meant she was home. When he finally knocked, the sound felt louder than it should have.

Jasmine opened the door a moment later. Her expression shifted the instant she saw him—shock first, then something fragile and hopeful she didn't bother trying to hide. "Mason," she said on a breath.

Mason took her in. Her curls were pulled into a bun, and she wore a T-shirt that read "Trust Me, I'm an Accountant" with simple shorts. The laid-back look matched his own casual shirt and jeans—and somehow made her even more beautiful to him.

"We need to talk," he whispered. She stepped aside without a word. The house smelled like tea and something citrusy. Clean. Intentional. Very her. Mason stayed standing while she closed the door behind him, both of them unsure where to put their hands, their eyes, the weight of everything unsaid. "I know what my mother did." Jasmine stilled. "And I know what she found—or thought she found."

Her shoulders sagged, like the fight had drained out of her all at once. "I'm not sure why I'm surprised."

"How long were you planning to let me believe you didn't trust me?" he asked. Not accusing. Just tired.

She swallowed. "I thought it was kinder."

He shook his head slightly. "You don't get to decide that for me." Silence stretched between them, thick but not hostile. "Why didn't you tell me?" Mason asked. "About your father, or what happened. You made it seem like he died from an accident or illness. You lied by omission."

Jasmine moved toward the kitchen, more out of habit than intention, then stopped and turned back to him. "Because that world isn't mine. It never was. And I've spent my entire adult life making sure it stayed that way."

"That doesn't answer the question."

She nodded. "I know." Jasmine took a breath, steadying herself. "My father built his life on shortcuts. On lies. On taking from people who didn't know better—or did and were too desperate to care. I grew up watching it. I hated it. But when I was eight, I started to help him."

Mason didn't interrupt.

"By sixteen, I understood what I was doing was wrong," she said quickly. "He needed someone to deliver paperwork. I knew it wasn't clean, but I didn't understand how bad it was until after. When it fell apart, he told me I was lucky. That I'd learned early." Her hands twisted together. "That was the first time I felt ashamed of myself."

Mason leaned against the wall, listening.

"After my mother died, he was all I had, but he was never there. He paid the bills and left me to raise myself. When I turned eighteen, I was going to be on the first thing smoking, and then he offered to pay for my college. I jumped at the chance to get out of there and truly be on my own. Every time we argued—every time I pulled away—he'd remind me about what he'd done for me. Like it was a leash. He could left me, after my mom died, and never come back. Lived his life the way he truly wanted to, but he made sure I was taken care of in his own way and I felt I owed him."

Her voice wavered, but she didn't stop. "I worked hard to clear my conscience. I chose a different life. Different values. Different people. I didn't lie about who I am—but I didn't lead with the worst parts of where I came from either."

Mason nodded slowly. "And the murder?"

Her lips pressed together, and there was a long pause. "By the time it happened, we barely spoke. I grieved the idea of a father, not the man he actually was. And I didn't want his death to become my defining story. I didn't want to tell you about the worst part of me. About the real reason I was at the gala that night we met."

He understood that more than he wanted to admit. "So why not tell me once my mother interfered?"

Jasmine's eyes filled. "Because I panicked. Because she threatened to make it look like I was hiding something bigger. And if I told you I'd helped him—even if you were never a target—it would make whatever evidence she created feel ... plausible." She laughed softly, bitter. "I convinced myself leaving was the lesser evil."

Mason straightened. "You were miserable."

"Yes," she whispered. "Every day."

He studied her then—not for flaws, but for truth. For the woman who'd been steady and kind and quietly brilliant. The woman who had, apparently, helped him more than once without asking for credit.

"You know," he said slowly, "I hired my own PI. I would never trust a thing my mother told me. He mentioned something interesting." Her brows knitted together. "He said you'd crossed paths with my company before. Indirectly. Consulting work. Before the night of the gala."

Jasmine's eyes widened. "You know about that?"

"I do now," Mason said. "You helped expose a vendor we were about to sign. Saved us millions."

She looked down. "I didn't want you to know it was me."

"Why? You made me think that auditing consulting work was my own idea."

"Because I didn't want you to think I was trying to earn something, and it was a work assignment, not my own idea."

Mason exhaled. "You give me less credit than I deserve."

She met his gaze. "And you give me more."

"No," he said gently. "I give you exactly what you've earned." The tension in the room shifted—easing, not disappearing, but softening into something manageable. "I'm not my mother," Mason said. "And you're not your father. I know what it's like to spend your life outrunning someone else's damage."

Her eyes glistened. "Then you understand why I was scared."

"I do," he said. "I just wish you'd trusted me enough to stand with you instead of walking away alone."

"I know, Kiera said as much but my own fear told me running was better."

"Can I trust you to put your track shoes away?"

Jasmine nodded. "I want to fight for us now, if it's not too late? If you'll let me."

Mason didn't hesitate. "I'm here, and I will fight for us too."

They stood there, no grand gestures, no sweeping promises—just honesty, finally unburdened. Free from lies. And for the first time in weeks, Mason was certain. They weren't starting over. They were starting clean.

Jasmine didn't remember who moved first. One moment, they were standing there, the weight of truth still hanging between them, and the next, Mason's hand was at her waist—steady, grounding, like no time had passed. She inhaled sharply, the contact undoing something tight and aching in her chest. His touch was like what she imagined being on drugs was like. She felt weightless, free, happy. Everything set her on fire; even his breath against her neck made her want to fall apart in his arms.

"Tell me to stop," he murmured, his forehead resting against hers.

She shook her head, tears clinging to her lashes. "Don't stop, ever."

That was all it took. His mouth found hers, not tentative—wildly certain. Like a decision already made. The kiss wasn't careful. It was full of everything they'd held back: relief, want, anger that had nowhere else to go. Jasmine clutched his jacket, fingers curling as if she were afraid he might disappear if she let go.

Mason kissed her like he meant to stay. When he pulled back, it was only far enough to look at her, his thumb brushing beneath her eye. "I missed you."

"I missed you." Staring into his eyes, she repeated it again. That broke whatever restraint he had left. They moved together instinctively, hands exploring familiar places with new urgency, relearning each other without the distance that had crept in before. Mason lifted her easily, carrying her down the hall as if it were the most natural thing in the world, as if this—*them*—had never been in question.

In the bedroom, the world narrowed to warmth and touch and the sound of their breathing. Clothes were discarded without thought, without ceremony. Mason traced the line of her breasts, her throat, as if he were memorizing her all over again. he said against her skin. "This is me choosing you."

She met his gaze, vulnerable and unguarded. "Choose me again tomorrow."

His answer was in the way he held her—secure, reverent, unhurried. In the way they came together not to escape what they'd faced, but to affirm it. There was no pretending here. No lies left between them. Just trust, rebuilt in touches and whispered promises.

Later, when the room was quiet and the air felt softer, Jasmine lay curled against his chest, listening to his heartbeat steady beneath her ear. "We'll mess up," she said sleepily.

Mason kissed the top of her head. “Probably.”

She smiled. “We’ll fight.”

“Definitely.”

“And we’ll choose each other anyway?”

His arms tightened around her, certain. “Every time.”

And for the first time in a long while, Jasmine believed it.

CHAPTER 9

Jasmine had learned to love the quiet hours.

Early mornings, late nights—those were when the numbers spoke most clearly. When there was no one watching, no one doubting, no one expecting her to prove she belonged in rooms she was only just beginning to enter. Her dining table had become her temporary office, neatly organized stacks of files replacing place settings, her laptop glowing softly as she worked through balance sheets and ledgers with practiced focus.

The advice Mason had given her—offered casually one night at dinner, like it hadn't fundamentally shifted her trajectory—had turned out to be brilliant.

Don't just offer accounting, he'd said. *Offer answers.*

Auditing. Independent, discreet audits for high-net-worth clients who wanted clarity without exposure. It was niche. It was needed. And, as it turned out, it was exactly what Jasmine was good at. Before, she had the backing of her company, but this was all her.

She'd started small—a handful of wealthy clients referred quietly through Mason and old contacts she'd helped in the past. Old-money types who preferred discretion over drama. She'd gone through their finances meticulously, not looking to accuse—just to understand. In two cases, she'd found inefficiencies so deeply embedded no one else had questioned them. Outdated structures. Redundant fees. Lazy assumptions.

Saving people money had a way of earning trust quickly.

By the third client, she felt it—that subtle shift from *trying* to build something to *actually* building it. Her firm was no longer a hopeful idea scribbled in a notebook. It was becoming real. She could do this; it was within her reach.

Then Jeremy Billups called.

She recognized the name instantly. Mason had mentioned him before—sharp, charismatic, self-made. The kind of man who built things from the ground up and trusted only his inner circle.

"Jasmine," Jeremy said over the phone, his tone careful. "I was hoping you might help me with something. Quietly."

Her fingers stilled over the keyboard. "Of course."

"I think my accountant is stealing from me."

There was no drama in his voice. Just unease. The kind that came from trusting someone for a long time and realizing, slowly, that something no longer lined up. Jasmine agreed to the audit that same day.

What she found took weeks. At first, it was subtle—minor discrepancies buried beneath legitimate transactions. Fees rounded up. Payments duplicated but mislabeled. Nothing obvious enough to trigger alarms, but enough to make her pause. She mapped everything out, tracing money through layers of accounts, reconstructing years of financial movement piece by piece.

The deeper she went, the worse it became. It wasn't sloppy theft. It was deliberate. Methodical. Designed to look like business as usual. The accountant—Jeremy's longtime friend—had been skimming for years. Small amounts at first, then bolder ones as confidence grew. Shell accounts. Falsified reports. A pattern that only emerged if you knew exactly where to look.

Jasmine sat back in her chair late one night, stomach heavy. She'd figured it out. How much? How long? And there was no way to unsee it. When she met Jeremy to go over her findings, she didn't soften the truth. She laid it out cleanly and professionally, the evidence organized and undeniable. She watched his face as realization settled in—not anger first, but hurt.

"I trusted him," he whispered.

"I know," Jasmine said. "That's why it worked."

He nodded slowly, absorbing it. Then he looked at her with respect. "You did this on your own—no one else knows about this?"

"Yes."

Jeremy exhaled. "I don't even know how to thank you."

"Any friend of Mason's is a friend of mine."

He nodded. Jeremy took her report—every document, every annotated trail—to the police. There was no denying what had been done. Jasmine felt a strange mix of emotions watching it unfold. Sadness for Jeremy, whose loyalty had been used against him. Disgust at the level of corruption. And beneath it all, a quiet, steady pride. She had uncovered the truth. Not because someone handed it to her. Not because of who she knew, knowing Mason had gotten her the job, but figuring it out was her alone. Because she was good at what she did.

She closed her laptop and leaned back, exhaustion settling into her bones—but so did something else. Confidence. The kind that didn't need validation.

Her phone buzzed.

Mason: *Jeremy called. He said you were incredible.*

She smiled softly. This was only the beginning.

Jasmine picked her phone back up and stared at the screen for a moment before dialing Kiera.

She hadn't realized how long it had been since they'd last talked—*really* talked. Between her day job at the accounting firm and the investigation that had consumed her nights, life had narrowed into spreadsheets, files, and late hours hunched over her laptop until her eyes burned.

The phone rang twice. "Please tell me you're coming up for air," Kiera said the moment she answered.

"I am." Jasmine laughed, relief softening her shoulders. "You free?"

"Very."

"I'm coming over. I've got wine and chocolate, and we can check out that new Regina King movie that just started streaming."

"You had me at chocolate," Kiera said, laughing.

An hour later, Jasmine pulled into Kiera's driveway. The townhouse sat in a quiet pocket of Farmington Hills—tree-lined streets, warm porch lights, the kind of place that felt calm just pulling up to it. Kiera opened the door before Jasmine could knock, pulling her into a hug that lingered just long enough to feel grounding.

They settled onto the couch with cookies, chocolate, and full glasses of wine. The movie played in the background, largely ignored, as the night eased into something comfortable and familiar.

"So," Kiera said, glancing sideways at her. "You've been quiet lately. What's going on in that brain of yours?"

Jasmine exhaled and told her everything—the client, the paper trail, the betrayal woven so carefully it almost went unnoticed. She explained how the numbers didn't lie, how every detail led back to someone Jeremy trusted completely.

"That's messed up," Kiera said, shaking her head. "I can't imagine hurting someone I love like that."

Jasmine nodded. "Neither can I. But these are billionaires. I think the people doing the stealing convince themselves they're entitled. Or that the money won't be missed."

"Did the guy get arrested?" Kiera asked.

"I don't know. Jeremy said he was going to the police, but that's all I heard."

"Think it'll hit the news?"

Jasmine shook her head. "No. Jeremy will keep it discreet. He doesn't want people knowing someone in his inner circle took advantage of him. He's known for keeping his circle tight—I'm sure he wants to keep it that way."

Kiera studied her for a moment, then smiled. "Still … this is huge, Jas. You did this."

Jasmine took a sip of wine, letting the words settle. For the first time in a long while, she didn't deflect or downplay it. "Yeah," she whispered. "I did."

Kiera asked how things had been going since Mason and Jasmine had gotten back together.

"Like no time has passed," Jasmine said with a soft smile remembering their talks.

She'd told him about the gala, her confrontation with Jack, and more about her upbringing with her mother before she passed. In return, Mason had opened up about his father and his complicated relationship with Brandy. Sharing those pieces of their past had only brought them closer.

Some nights, Mason would come over with work, and they would sit together in comfortable silence—each focused on their own laptops, simply enjoying being in each other's presence. No pressure. No forced conversation. Just peace.

Kiera smiled at that. "That's how you know it's real. Best friend hook up is back on!"

Jasmine laughed.

Then her expression shifted. "How do you feel knowing Brandy could try something else?"

Jasmine hesitated. "I'm hopeful that now that there are no more secrets between Mason and me, it'll be different. We're stronger."

Kiera snorted. "Girl, that woman probably isn't above drugging her own son and planting a woman. So believe half of what you see and none of what you hear."

Jasmine laughed, but a small knot of fear still twisted in her stomach.

"I do worry she'll try again," Jasmine admitted. "But Mason and I can handle his mother. Now that he knows what she's capable of, we'll be more careful. He thinks eventually she'll move on to Tiffany—or someone else she thinks is more important."

Kiera raised a brow. "Let's hope she finds a new hobby. Preferably one that doesn't involve small Dalmatian puppies or ruining people's lives."

They sat there for a few hours, laughter replacing tension, the weight of the case finally lifting. As the night wound down, Jasmine felt something she hadn't let herself feel in weeks—balance. Tomorrow would bring more work, questions, maybe even consequences she couldn't yet see. But tonight, surrounded by comfort and honesty, she allowed herself to just *be*.

* * *

Brandy did not take failure well.

Mason may not have thought his girlfriend was a con woman, but their friends would. She would never hear the end of it if her friends found out. He had women knocking down his door and he picked her? He could do what he wanted, but she would not be welcomed in their circles.

Her gaze shifted to her daughter. Brandy's lips thinned. "I need you to do something."

Tiffany sat across from her, arms crossed, already wary. "Do what, exactly?"

"Nothing you can't handle. Take Mason's *girlfriend* out to lunch. You remind her where she stands," Brandy said coolly. "She is not family. And she never will be."

Tiffany's stomach tightened. "You want me to threaten her?"

"I want you to put her in her place. There's a difference."

"This isn't a mob boss movie, Mother. Just because I tell her she isn't welcome in this family, it won't make her break it off with Mason."

"It's not supposed to. I just want her to know where she stands with us. The more people who tell her they disapprove of this relationship, the better."

"You do know this will only piss Mason off if he finds out I took his girlfriend out and was mean to her."

"Do you think I care what Mason feels about this situation?" Brandy raised a sharply arched brow. Tiffany didn't respond right away. Brandy leaned forward, eyes sharp. "You're my daughter. You understand loyalty. Where does yours lie—with your brother or me?"

Tiffany forced a nod she didn't feel. "Fine. I'll handle it."

* * *

Jasmine almost dropped her phone when Tiffany's name popped up on the screen.

Hi Jasmine. Can we meet for lunch? Just us?

She read it twice, but still didn't know what to think. Was this another trap? Mason's sister felt like an unknown variable. Jasmine didn't want to want Tiffany on her side, but with his mother firmly in the no position, she felt like she could use a win. Mason told Jasmine Tiffany was a lot like their mother, but that she'd be a better person without their mother's influence.

I'd love that, she replied.

They met at a small bistro downtown, understated and quiet. Tiffany arrived first, posture stiff, expression carefully neutral. Jasmine greeted her with a warm smile that wasn't forced—just hopeful. The first thing Tiffany noticed was that her hair was different from the picture her mother showed her, where Jasmine had had braids.

Now Jasmine had curly hair that fell just past her ears, warm brown eyes, full lips, and a small, straight nose. She was taller than Tiffany's five-two frame—five-seven, maybe five-eight if Tiffany had to guess. There was nothing sharp or calculating about her appearance, she dressed cute in a off the rack type of way, nothing that screamed threat.

Her dress was a simple peach color, definitely not designer like the YSL suit Tiffany had on. Tiffany couldn't understand what her mother hated about this woman so much. And sitting there, watching her, she regretted all the times she had allowed her mother to bully her into choices she hadn't wanted—especially dating Dennis. His family was well connected, and her mother had loved how he looked on Tiffany's arm. He was Boris Kodjoe fine, charming, and generous with his money. But he loved drugs more.

Tiffany had convinced herself she could help him, that his habit was something she could manage if she tried hard enough. Her body was her temple—she would never touch anything that might compromise her mind or her beauty—but she believed she could save him anyway.

Leaving him hadn't been easy. When she told her mother about his addiction, she'd been told to let her and Dennis's mother "handle it." That solution lasted all of three months. By then, Dennis was back to doing lines, more volatile, more controlling—especially with the people who worked for him.

The day Tiffany tried to intervene, he slapped her and told her to stay in her place. She didn't remember everything clearly after that. She only remembered screaming at him, remembered his maid and butler trying to pull her off him. No one in her life had ever raised a hand to her like that. She hadn't even known she had it in her, but years of self-defense classes and bottled anger had her clinging to him like a koala bear, swinging until they dragged her away. That was the last time she'd taken dating advice from her mother—whose only response to the incident had been that they'd "find a better match next time."

She admired Mason for his refusal to let their mother dictate his life. In the beginning, Tiffany had tried to follow that same path, but it hadn't come easily. She hadn't known who to trust. Even people her age wanted proximity to her for what she represented, not who she was.

Adopting her mother's attitude had helped build the shell that kept her safe—but she was tired. Tired of the backstabbing, the manipulation, the constant mess that came with being rich. It was a good problem to have, she knew that, and she rarely complained. Still, days like this made her want to take her money and start over somewhere far away from the cruelty her mother wielded so casually.

She hadn't come here to do her mother's dirty work. She was here to form her own opinion. Because the woman her mother hated so much didn't look like a villain at all.

"Thanks for meeting me," Jasmine said as she sat.

"Of course," Tiffany replied, studying her. *This is who Mother hates so much?*

They ordered. Small talk followed—safe, polite, superficial. Tiffany waited for her opening, rehearsed words hovering on the tip of her tongue.

Then Jasmine spoke first. "Mason speaks very highly of you. Thank you for getting him to take another chance on me."

Tiffany stiffened. "That's one way to put it. I just told him to look out for himself."

Jasmine smiled faintly. "Right, that could have gone either way." Tiffany just nodded. "My father was controlling," Jasmine continued, wanting to explain herself. "Not physically. Just … everywhere else. In my choices. My future. Even when he wasn't around."

Tiffany's curiosity slipped past her defenses. "Was?"

"He died," Jasmine said quietly.

Tiffany had read the file her mother had, but wanted to hear from Jasmine. "I'm sorry," Tiffany said, surprised to mean it.

"It's complicated," Jasmine said. "We barely had a relationship. But he was still my only living parent." Her voice softened. "And losing him made everything final in a way I wasn't ready for."

Tiffany hesitated. "What about your mother?"

Jasmine's expression changed—gentler, sadder. "She died when I was young. Sometimes I think about how different my life would've been if she'd lived. I think she would've protected me. Balanced him out." Tiffany understood more than Jasmine knew. Jasmine met her eyes. "I worked hard to become someone separate from my father. I've made mistakes. I've paid for them. But everything I am now—I built it myself. I hope you will give me a chance to prove that."

The words landed heavier than Tiffany expected. "My mother likes to control outcomes," Tiffany said slowly. "People, too."

Jasmine nodded. "I know." There was no bitterness in it. No accusation. Just understanding. Silence settled between them—not awkward, but thoughtful.

"You know," Tiffany said finally, "I came here today because my mother asked me to." Jasmine's breath caught, but she didn't interrupt. "She wanted me to make it clear you weren't welcome. To scare you off."

Jasmine absorbed that quietly. "And?"

Tiffany let out a small, humorless laugh. "And now I'm sitting here realizing how familiar all of this feels." They shared a look—two women shaped by parents who mistook control for love. "I don't want to be another person standing against you. Or against Mason."

Relief washed through Jasmine, warm and unexpected. "Thank you. That means more than you know."

Tiffany smiled—real this time. "I think we might actually get along."

"I was hoping you'd say that."

One less enemy. One more ally. And for the first time, Jasmine believed that maybe this family wasn't entirely closed to her after all.

Lunch lingered longer than either of them had planned. The plates had been cleared, replaced by coffee neither woman was really drinking. Outside the restaurant, the afternoon moved on without them, but inside, something quieter and more consequential was unfolding.

Tiffany exhaled slowly, fingers tracing the rim of her cup. "There's something else you should understand about my mother." Jasmine didn't interrupt. She'd learned when silence was an invitation. "She's still the head of our family. *Our* only living parent. Everything—*everything*—runs through her. Shares. Influence. And Jewel Pharmaceuticals." She gave a tight smile. "That's the crown."

Jasmine's brows knit together. "You want to be CEO."

"I *will* be," Tiffany said, the certainty automatic. Then she softened. "If I play it right."

Jasmine absorbed that. "And playing it right means...?"

"Pretending," Tiffany said simply. "Pretending I agree with her. Pretending I don't see what she does to people. Pretending I don't question her version of love." Her jaw tightened. "If I push back too hard, she'll cut me off before I ever get close."

Jasmine nodded slowly. "Mason told you to walk away."

Tiffany laughed under her breath. "For years."

"He says freedom is worth more than a title."

"And he's right," Tiffany said. "For *him*." She met Jasmine's gaze. "But I've already paid too much. I grew up inside that machine. I bent when she wanted me to bend. I stayed quiet when I wanted to scream. I'm not starting over with nothing to show for it."

Tiffany couldn't believe how honest she was being, but she trusted Mason's judgement. Could feel this woman's genuine nature in the short time they'd spent here.

"That makes sense," Jasmine whispered.

Tiffany blinked. "You're not going to tell me to be brave?"

"No," Jasmine replied. "I'm going to tell you that you deserve what you've worked for." That surprised Tiffany. "This is your birthright. And wanting it doesn't make you weak. It means you survived long enough to claim it."

Tiffany's shoulders relaxed, just a fraction. "Thank you."

"I do think," Jasmine added carefully, "that living under someone else's thumb—forever—will cost you more than you realize."

Tiffany smiled faintly. "You sound like Mason."

Jasmine smiled. "He's hard to argue with."

"He is," Tiffany said. "But he didn't grow up knowing the board members by name. Or attending meetings before puberty. This life"—she gestured vaguely—"it's all I've ever known."

Jasmine studied her then, seeing past the designer clothes, the practiced confidence, the subtle entitlement that came from never having to worry about survival. Tiffany *was* spoiled. Sheltered in ways Jasmine had never been. But she wasn't cruel. And she wasn't empty.

"I can tell you have a good heart," Jasmine whispered.

Tiffany scoffed. "Buried under years of privilege and denial."

"Still there," Jasmine said. "Mason has it too. Same core. You just learned different armor."

Something softened in Tiffany's expression. "You really believe that?"

"I do."

They sat with that for a moment.

"I'll have to keep pretending with my mother," Tiffany said eventually. "At least for now. She can't know we talked like this. Or that I don't see you the way she wants me to."

"I understand and agree," Jasmine said without hesitation.

"And," Tiffany added, "if she pushes too hard—if she crosses another line—you two have a woman on the inside."

Jasmine smiled. "Good to know."

When they stood to leave, Tiffany hesitated, then pulled Jasmine into a brief, awkward hug. "I'm glad Mason didn't let her scare you off."

"So am I."

As Jasmine walked away, Tiffany felt something shift again—not dramatically, not completely—but enough. She wasn't free yet. But she wasn't blind either. And sometimes, that was how change began.

* * *

Tiffany waited at her childhood home for the butler—really more of a house manager—to open the door. The place still smelled the same: polished wood, expensive candles, and a faint trace of control. Some things never changed.

Her mother had summoned her the moment she'd returned to town from her business trip, eager to hear how lunch with Jasmine had gone. Tiffany chuckled quietly to herself as she stepped inside. It was pure madness that Brandy thought a lunch invitation laced with *you're not welcome here* mean-girl energy would send Jasmine running. If anything, it only made Tiffany more curious.

Mason had disapproved of plenty of men in Tiffany's life, and she'd never cared what he thought—never once let his opinion sway her choices. So why would her disapproval matter to him or Jasmine?

Because her mother's hatred felt irrational. Personal.

Brandy sat in the living room, perfectly composed, legs crossed, tablet resting on her lap like a judge waiting to pass sentence. "Well? How did it go?"

"Fine," Tiffany said smoothly, settling into the chair across from her. "Just lunch."

Brandy finally looked up. "And her?"

Tiffany paused just long enough to seem thoughtful. *You're really asking me to confirm this ridiculousness?* "She's… interesting."

Brandy nodded. "That's what I thought. Very calculated."

Tiffany resisted the urge to roll her eyes. *Calculated? Or just not intimidated by you?* Instead, she gave a small, knowing smile. "She definitely knows how to present herself."

"Exactly," Brandy said. "Women like that always do."

Tiffany hummed in agreement, even as her stomach tightened. *Women like that*—as if competence were a crime. As if Jasmine's biggest offense was not shrinking.

"She didn't strike me as reckless," Tiffany added carefully. "But I can see why you'd want to be cautious."

Brandy relaxed a fraction. "Mason is vulnerable right now."

No, Tiffany thought. *He's just outside your reach.* "I understand," Tiffany said. "You're just trying to protect him."

"That's all I've ever done."

Tiffany nodded, playing her part flawlessly. Inside, though, she was cataloging every contradiction, every familiar manipulation. This wasn't concern—it was control dressed up as love.

"So," Brandy said, "you agree she's not right for him."

Tiffany offered a diplomatic smile. "I think it's too soon to tell. But I trust your instincts." *Even when they're rooted in jealousy and fear.*

They talked about the lunch a little longer, Tiffany agreeing with Brandy all the way.

Brandy seemed satisfied with that and went on to tell Tiffany all the reasons Jasmine didn't 'fit'. Tiffany felt the familiar exhaustion settle in—the cost of pretending, of masking herself to keep the peace. But she also felt something else: clarity.

Her mother wasn't protecting Mason. She was threatened. And no amount of polite agreement would change the fact that Brandy's behavior was spiraling into something desperate. Tiffany came to a quiet realization as she sat there nodding along to her mother's complaints: Brandy didn't want Jasmine gone. She wanted her *manageable*. Bendable. Moveable.

In their social circle, people understood appearance and hierarchy. There were rules—unspoken but rigid—about who led and who followed. Brandy had expected Mason to choose a woman with "breeding," someone who knew how things worked, who would fall in line, follow Brandy's lead, and in doing so keep Mason exactly where she wanted him. Under her control.

Jasmine disrupted that balance simply by existing. She didn't seek approval. She didn't defer. And Mason being in love only made it worse—it pushed Brandy to the outside, where Mason kept her instead of at the center of his decisions. This wasn't about Brandy fearing that Mason had fallen for someone who didn't love him. It wasn't about protecting the family money or reputation. It was about losing the control she once had over her son.

Brandy saw it clearly—how deeply Mason loved Jasmine—just as Tiffany had seen how deeply Jasmine loved Mason in return. What Brandy didn't yet understand was that it was already too late. That ship had sailed. Mason and Jasmine were together, firmly and by choice. And no matter how much pressure Brandy applied, no matter how many social games she played, there was nothing she could do to change that. For the first time, Tiffany felt certain of it. Control was no longer on the table.

Brandy finally finished her rant, her voice clipped with irritation. "I'll make sure everyone knows. She won't feel welcome anywhere."

Tiffany frowned, a flicker of panic cutting through her practiced calm. She couldn't let that happen. "I wouldn't do that, Mother," Tiffany said gently, shaking her head. "For one, it would get back to Mason." Brandy scoffed, but Tiffany pressed on before she could interrupt. "And two," Tiffany added, lowering her voice just enough to sound concerned rather than defiant, "it could make *us* look bad. Being associated with that type of behavior? A con woman, in our circle. People would talk. We'd be the laughingstock—and we'd never live it down, even if Mason left her."

That gave Brandy pause. She leaned back, lips pursed, thinking it through. Tiffany watched the calculation settle in, relief and unease tangling in her chest. Brandy hated nothing more than losing social footing. "You're right," Brandy said finally. "The last thing I need is the power dynamic shifting because of *her*." Tiffany nodded, masking her relief. Brandy's fingers tightened around her tablet. "I'll keep everything the PI found locked away. No need to be reckless."

Brandy agreed—there was no need to make their lives difficult.

She hated to admit it, but she had gone about this all wrong. Forcing Jasmine out would only push Mason closer to her. He was blinded by love and Payless shoes.

Getting rid of the girl by pressure and threats had backfired.

So she would change tactics. She would play nice.

Lower Jasmine's guard. Smile in her face. Play nice but not too nice. Extend invitations. Offer olive branches wrapped in silk and poison. Make herself look reasonable, supportive—even unconcerned.

Maybe, with enough "breeding," she could mold the girl into something presentable.

The thought made Brandy's skin crawl. She didn't want to fix Jasmine.

She wanted her gone.

But Brandy was smart enough to recognize when the game had shifted.

This was no longer a war of force. It was a war of patience.

"We shall play nice… for now."

For now, Tiffany thought. As Brandy dismissed the conversation, Tiffany knew better than to relax. Her mother wasn't finished—just delayed. Brandy had never accepted defeat gracefully. She would find another way to get rid of Jasmine. And whatever that way was, she just hoped Mason and herself could stop it.

CHAPTER 10

Mason sat in Terrence's cigar room as they smoked and played poker, the air thick with cedar and familiarity. What had started as a bi-weekly ritual in college had survived adulthood, though now it was more like once a month—careers, families, and responsibilities pulling them in different directions.

Terrence, only ten years older than Tank and Mason, had always felt less like a peer and more like a steady presence. After Mason lost his father, Terrence—and his father, Carlton—had become the honest, grounding male figures he'd needed. They spoke plainly, listened without judgment, and never tried to control him. Tank had come along almost by accident. He'd found the Knights far less critical than his own father, and somewhere between late-night talks and bad poker hands, they'd all bonded.

Now, as grown men, the rhythm remained.

Mason studied his cards longer than necessary, his mind elsewhere. He hesitated only a moment before finally saying what had been sitting heavy on his chest. "I'm going to ask Jasmine to marry me."

Terrence looked up first, a slow smile spreading across his face. Tank froze mid-shuffle. "Well damn," Tank said.

Mason chuckled, but the seriousness in his eyes didn't waver. "We've been back together almost six months, and I can't imagine being happier."

He and Jasmine were stronger than ever. They talked through everything. No secrets. No games. Jasmine was tired of Brandy's campaign to push her out, and Mason didn't blame her. He'd stopped their monthly dinners without hesitation and even offered to go no contact if that's what she needed.

She'd refused. "As long as we only have to deal with her sparingly," Jasmine had told him. "Holidays, maybe. I can manage that." She liked Tiffany. Wanted to protect that bond. Wanted open communication, family—even when it would've been easier to draw hard lines. Mason loved her for that. Even when she had every right to ask him to cut his mother off completely, she didn't.

Brandy had been strangely quiet and accepting of these changes.

Terrence leaned back in his chair, studying Mason through the smoke. "You sure you're ready for what that'll stir up?"

Mason didn't hesitate this time. "I'm sure about her."

Tank raised his glass. "Then that's all that matters." Mason nodded, feeling something settle in his chest. The future felt clear.

Terrance set his glass down. "Okay. First things first—prenup."

Tank nodded emphatically. "Ironclad. Romantic doesn't mean stupid."

Mason rolled his eyes. "I knew that was coming."

"I'm not saying don't marry her," Terrance said. "I'm saying protect what you've built. For *both* of you."

Tank leaned forward. "Actually, make it a partnership. Transparency. Assets. Expectations. You don't want money poisoning what's good."

Mason had considered that. "She'd want that, and I don't disagree with either of you, I plan to meet with my lawyer Monday."

"That's how you know she's the right one," Terrance said. "The right woman doesn't flinch at hard conversations."

Mason's phone buzzed on the table. Jasmine's name lit the screen, and his mouth softened instinctively. Tank caught it and grinned. "Yeah. You're done for." Mason didn't argue. Tank took a long pull from his beer, then squinted at Mason like he was trying to read fine print on a bad contract. "You're serious," he said finally. "You're actually going to do it."

Mason didn't hesitate. "Yeah."

Terrance let out a low whistle. "I remember when your biggest commitment issue was buying furniture. Welcome to the club my brother."

"That couch was ugly," Mason muttered.

Tank laughed. "That couch lasted longer than most marriages, so don't knock it."

As they sat around Terrance's table Mason felt completely at home. Years of bad decisions, good advice, and worse hangovers had taken place there. If Mason was going to talk marriage anywhere, this was the place.

Terrance leaned forward. "Now, proposal strategy. Don't overproduce it."

Tank snapped his fingers. "Yes. No flash mobs."

"Definitely no flash mobs," Terrance said. "If strangers clap afterward, you've done it wrong."

Mason snorted. "I wasn't planning a parade."

"Good," Tank said. "Because she strikes me as a private-moment person. Meaningful. Intentional."

Terrance pointed at him. "Also—say something real. Not just 'will you marry me?' Tell her *why*. Women like context."

"Speak for yourself," Tank said. "I like context too."

Mason smiled faintly. "I already know what I'd say."

Tank's expression softened. "That's how you know."

Terrance lifted his glass. "One more thing—and this is the important part."

Mason looked at him. "Go on."

"Marriage isn't ownership," Terrance said. "It's a partnership. Two people choosing each other over and over again, even when it's inconvenient."

Tank nodded. "Especially when it's inconvenient."

"And when your mother is involved," Terrance added dryly.

Tank laughed. "Man, marrying her is already an act of rebellion. I respect it."

Mason chuckled, shaking his head. "She makes me want to be better."

Tank raised his beer. "That's the whole game right there." They clinked bottles, the moment easy and familiar. "Just promise us one thing," Tank said.

"What?"

"Once you're married," Terrance said, "you'll still show up for poker night."

"And if she ever drives you crazy," Tank continued, "you come here first before doing something stupid."

Mason smirked. "Deal."

Tank grinned. "Alright then. When you propose, send pictures."

Terrance shook his head. "No—send video. I want to see her face and if Mason cries."

Mason laughed, a deep, steady sound. "She's going to say yes."

Tank leaned back, satisfied. "Then Congratulations my brother."

Terrance raised his beer. "Congratulations."

Mason grinned; he was getting engaged.

* * *

The dream came hard and fast, like a door kicked in. Jasmine was running—barefoot, breath tearing out of her chest as shadows stretched too long behind her. Her father's voice echoed down a narrow hallway she didn't recognize, sharp and furious and desperate all at once. *You owe me.*

She turned a corner and found him standing there, younger than she remembered but angrier, his eyes too bright. Papers were scattered at his feet. Numbers. Contracts. Names she didn't want to see. "I tried," she told him, panic clawing at her throat. "I tried to fix it."

He stepped closer. "You don't get to walk away."

"No," she whispered, backing up. "I did."

His hand reached for her—

And she screamed.

Mason was awake before the sound fully left her mouth. "Jasmine," he said, pulling her upright as she thrashed. "Hey. It's okay. You're here. You're with me."

Her eyes were wild, unfocused. "Mason?"

"I know," he murmured, holding her firmly. "You're safe."

She collapsed against him, shaking, breath coming in sharp gasps as reality slowly replaced the dream. Mason felt her heart racing under his palm, too fast, too frantic. He held her until the tremors eased, until her breathing slowed and her body stopped bracing for a blow that wasn't coming.

But he didn't relax, because this wasn't nothing. Jasmine had spoken about her mother often—fondly, painfully, like a wound that never quite closed but had been tended to with care. Her mother was memory and love and loss, all braided together.

Her father was silence. And now that silence was screaming.

"You don't have to tell me," Mason said quietly after a long moment. "But I'm here."

She nodded against his chest, exhaustion pulling her back under. Within minutes, she was asleep again. Mason wasn't. He stared at the ceiling, a familiar dread settling in his gut. He recognized this pattern too well. The mind burying pain until it demanded to be seen. Nightmares were never random. They were messages. And Jasmine had been carrying hers alone for far too long.

The next morning, sunlight filtered into the kitchen as Jasmine poured coffee, moving carefully, like the night had left her bruised in ways she didn't want to acknowledge.

Mason watched her for a moment before speaking. "About last night …"

She stiffened almost imperceptibly. "It was just a bad dream."

"Maybe, but it felt bigger than that."

She turned, mug in hand. "I don't want to make it a thing."

"That's kind of my concern," he replied softly.

Jasmine sighed, sitting across from him. "Mason, I've dealt with my past. I'm fine."

He held her gaze. "You've dealt with some of it. You've buried the rest."

Her jaw tightened. "You don't know that."

"I do," he said calmly. "Because I did the same thing." That got her attention. "My father's death wrecked me. Not right away; I stayed functional. Productive. Everyone thought I was handling it." He gave a humorless smile. "I wasn't." She listened now, quiet. "I didn't start therapy until years later, and by then, I was angry all the time. Closed off. Reacting to things I didn't understand." He paused. "It helped. More than I ever expected."

Jasmine wrapped both hands around her mug. "I don't like the idea of digging all that up."

"I know," he said. "But ignoring it doesn't make it disappear. It just waits." She looked down, thinking. "You talk about your mother. You let yourself miss her. You grieve her openly. But you never talk about your father—not his death, not what he did to you, not what you lost or didn't lose."

"I did tell you those things."

"We shared with each other, but you need to get professional help. Someone that can get these feelings stored in the right place."

Her throat worked. "It's complicated and I don't like thinking about these things."

"All the more reason," Mason said.

Silence stretched between them. Jasmine's eyes glistened, but she didn't cry. "I don't want him to have any more space in my life."

"I get that. But this isn't about him. It's about you."

She exhaled slowly, shoulders slumping. "I'm not promising anything."

"I'm not asking for a promise. Just that you'll think about it."

She nodded once. "I will."

Mason reached across the table and took her hand. "You don't have to carry this alone. Not anymore."

She squeezed his fingers, a small but genuine smile breaking through. "I'll give it more thought."

It wasn't a yes, but it wasn't a no.

* * *

Jasmine walked into Walter's looking effortless in her tailored gray business suit, briefcase in hand. Her curls bounced softly as she scanned the room, twisting back and forth with each step. The low lighting and muted jazz gave the space an intimate hum, the kind of place people came to be seen without being obvious about it.

Walter's was a trendy speakeasy with a secret menu and a reputation for fun. Jasmine would've happily dined here for pleasure, but tonight was strictly business. Jeremy had called earlier that week, making introductions to a family friend who needed her assistance. Jasmine hadn't hesitated. She wasn't swamped yet, but the work was steady—enough to remind her that she was building something real. Step by step, she was moving closer to the life she'd envisioned for herself.

Her eyes caught a raised hand near the back of the restaurant. Jasmine smiled and made her way toward the table. The man waiting for her looked to be in his late fifties, pleasant and composed. His hair was gray, neatly cut, and his beard matched—trimmed close, intentional. His skin was the warm shade of butterscotch, smooth despite the years. Rich brown eyes assessed her with curiosity rather than judgment, and his full lips curved into an easy smile as she approached.

"Ms. Franklin?" he asked, rising from his seat.

"Yes," Jasmine replied, extending her hand. "And you must be Mr. Wallace."

"Please—Calvin," he said, shaking her hand firmly. "Jeremy spoke very highly of you."

"Likewise," Jasmine said, taking her seat when he pulled out the chair for her. "He said you were someone who values clarity."

Calvin chuckled. "That's a polite way of saying I don't like surprises."

"Then we'll get along just fine," Jasmine said.

They ordered drinks—sparkling water for Jasmine, bourbon for Calvin—and she listened as he explained his situation. A family trust. Long-standing investments. Numbers that didn't quite line up the way they should. Jasmine asked thoughtful questions, flipping open her briefcase with practiced ease she got her note pad and pen. She didn't rush him or interrupt. She simply listened, absorbing the details, already seeing patterns form.

"I want the truth," Calvin said finally. "Even if it's uncomfortable."

Jasmine met his gaze, calm and confident. "That's the only way I work."

A slow smile spread across his face. "I had a feeling Jeremy sent me the right person."

As they talked, Jasmine felt that familiar spark—the quiet satisfaction of being exactly where she was meant to be. This wasn't luck. This wasn't timing. This was her craft. And she was getting very good at it. They discussed Jasmine's rate and a few final details before wrapping up their business.

Calvin nodded, clearly satisfied. "I'll expect weekly updates."

"You'll have them. Thank you for your time."

After they parted ways, Jasmine excused herself to the restroom to freshen up before leaving. The evening had gone well—productive, promising—and she wanted to walk out composed, not rushed. She was washing her hands when the door opened and two women walked in. Both were impeccably styled—faces perfectly made up, bodies surgically enhanced, designer handbags resting on manicured hands. Their clothes were unmistakably expensive. Their expressions, unmistakably sour the moment they spotted Jasmine. Her instincts kicked in immediately. She didn't recognize them, which meant only one thing: Mason or Brandy. Neither option sat well with her.

The blonde—green-eyed, tall, sharp—moved toward the mirror to reapply her lipstick while the other woman, shorter with deep brown skin and long black hair, positioned herself near the door like a lookout.

Jasmine rinsed the soap from her hands quickly. She was so not in the mood for this. The blonde paused mid-application and stared at Jasmine through the mirror.

"You're dating Mason Jewel, aren't you?"

Mason, dang it. If she were a betting woman she totally would of bet Brandy.

Jasmine dried her hands slowly, meeting the woman's gaze in the reflection. Her first instinct was to deny it—watch them scramble, confused—but tonight, she chose honesty. "I am."

The blonde smirked. "How'd someone like *you* pull that off?"

The other woman snickered. Jasmine chuckled, the absurdity almost impressive. *Is this really going to be my life?* Being cornered in bathrooms by women who felt entitled to assess her worth? The flicker of panic and grief passed quickly. Mason was worth it. Every bit of it. He loved her fully—even her worst habits, even her stinky socks. A man who loved and affirmed her the way he did was worth standing her ground for.

She mentally rolled up her sleeves. "Wouldn't you love to know?" Jasmine said sweetly. "I can tell you this—it's not all that plastic surgery you've had that would get him."

Both women gasped in unison. "I'm guessing by that Target suit," the blonde said, "he likes something more … understated?"

Before Jasmine could respond, the bathroom door opened again. Tiffany walked in. She let the door close behind her before her eyes moved from Jasmine to the two women, lingering just long enough to make them uncomfortable.

"Hi, Tiffany," the shorter woman said quickly. "You look great tonight."

"I agree," the blonde added. "Is that the new Balmain slingbacks? I didn't know they were out yet."

Tiffany was stunning in a light pink business suit with a pleated skirt, black handbag, and matching shoes. She acknowledged only the blonde, ignoring the other woman entirely. "I can tell by the tension in here that you came to be messy," Tiffany said calmly. "Let me save you the trouble. Jasmine isn't just in a relationship with Mason—she's my friend." Her tone sharpened. "If I hear you—or any of your clones—say one word in my presence or anyone else's, and it gets back to me, you will regret it. Deeply. Are we clear?"

The blonde looked terrified—so much so Jasmine would've thought Tiffany was holding a gun to her head. "Sorry, Tiffany," she said quickly. "We thought she wasn't welcome. I must've misunderstood."

Tiffany took a step closer. "We Jewels don't take kindly to assumptions. Why don't you speak to Brandy and make sure you spread the word—Jasmine is off limits."

"Yes." The blonde nodded frantically. "No problem. I'll make sure everyone knows." She glanced at Jasmine, suddenly contrite. "I'm PMSing. Forgive me."

And just like that, they hurried out. Jasmine burst into laughter the moment the door closed. "Brandy isn't my biggest fan. I don't think sending them her way will help my case."

Tiffany laughed too. "Those girls would have their fingernails pulled out before they ever speak to my mother."

Jasmine laughed even harder. "Thank you. That could've gotten ugly."

"I saw them watching you all night, Berk has always had a thing for Mason." Tiffany said. "When you got up, so did they. I knew exactly what they were up to."

Jasmine smiled. "You've been here this whole time? I didn't even see you—and you're hard to miss in that outfit."

Tiffany batted her lashes. "VIP section, girl. You can't see me, but I can see *you*."

They talked a little longer before Tiffany excused herself to return to her date. As Jasmine left the restroom, her heart felt lighter. Having Tiffany on her side changed everything. Maybe fighting for Mason wouldn't be as hard as she'd thought.

* * *

The call from his mother came two days later.

"Mason," Brandy said brightly. "I was thinking it's time we all spent some quality time together. Jasmine and I barely know each other."

Mason rolled his eyes. "Are you being serious right now?"

"What's done is done. Let's not dwell on the past, dear."

His jaw tightened. "What are you suggesting?"

"A family vacation," she replied smoothly. "The Dominican Republic. Sun, relaxation. A fresh start."

Mason almost laughed. He knew better. But he also knew exactly what he wanted. "That sounds great."

There was a pause—brief, suspicious. "I'm glad you agree," Brandy said. "I'll handle the arrangements."

After he hung up, Mason smiled to himself. He hadn't said yes because he trusted her. He'd said yes because he was going to propose and the Dominican Republic would be the perfect place. And nothing would unsettle his mother more than that. He just hoped Jasmine would be on board.

He dialed Tiffany immediately. "She invited us to the Dominican," he said without preamble. "What's she planning?"

Tiffany sighed. "If I knew, I'd tell you. She hasn't said a word to me."

"So no secret ambush?"

"Not that I'm aware of," Tiffany replied. Then, after a beat, "But I'll come, so we can keep an eye on her."

Mason smirked and told her his plans to propose. Tiffany was growing up; he could see cracks in her exterior he couldn't see before. She wasn't like their mother, and she had more of their father than she would like to admit.

"I really thought I'd get married first," she said cheerfully. "I want a front-row seat when you propose; Mother might pop a blood vessel."

He laughed. "She will be mad, but that's only the second-best thing that will happen on this trip."

"Well then," Tiffany replied. "I'll bring popcorn."

Mason ended the call, phone warm in his hand, heart steady. The timing was perfect, but the circumstances weren't ideal. And whatever storms waited for them in paradise, Mason was ready to face them—ring in hand.

* * *

Brandy hung up the phone and sat perfectly still, her fingers tightening around it as resolve settled in her chest. This was the last chance. She would reason with the girl one more time. Appeal to logic. Offer money if she had to—generously, discreetly. Everyone had a price, whether they admitted it or not. And if Jasmine was as smart as she claimed to be, she'd know when to take the deal and walk away.

Brandy had never felt so out of the loop in her life. Because of Jasmine, the monthly dinners had stopped. Mason showed up to board meetings like an obligation rather than an extension of her authority. And anytime she tried to bring Jasmine up—casually, carefully—he shut her down without discussion.

It confirmed what Brandy had known all along. Jasmine was poisoning him against her. Turning him. Whispering things that made him question her intentions, her guidance, her place in his life. Brandy had raised Mason. Molded him. Positioned him exactly where he was supposed to be. She would not stand by and watch some woman undo decades of work under the guise of love. Absolutely not.

This upcoming trip was her opportunity. Neutral ground. Fewer eyes. A controlled environment. If this attempt failed—if Jasmine proved stubborn or greedy or foolish—then Brandy would be forced to consider alternatives. Less pleasant ones.

She stood, smoothing the front of her blouse, her face already settling into a mask of calm sophistication. One way or another, Jasmine would be removed. Brandy Jewel had never lost control of her family before. And she wasn't about to start now.

CHAPTER 11

Jasmine stood by the window, phone pressed to her ear, watching the black SUV idle at the curb. "I'm really not excited about this," she whispered.

Kiera laughed on the other end of the line. "You're flying to a private island on a private jet with the man you love. Forgive me if my sympathy is limited."

"That's not the part I'm dreading," Jasmine muttered. "It's his mother. A weekend of forced smiles and passive aggression, or regular aggression with Brandy I can't be sure."

"Ah," Kiera said knowingly. "The final boss."

Jasmine sighed. "Exactly."

There was a pause, then Kiera's voice softened. "Okay, but hear me out. You. Mason. Sun. Luxury. And the added bonus of existing happily in Brandy's presence purely out of spite."

Jasmine snorted despite herself. "You sound like Mason and you both make a compelling argument."

"I always do," Kiera replied. "Besides, haven't you been working nonstop?"

Jasmine glanced at the neatly stacked folders on her desk. "Jeremy's referrals alone doubled my workload. I'm exhausted—but it's a good exhausted."

"You're building something real," Kiera said. "You should be proud."

"I am. I'm not ready to officially launch yet, but I've got a solid starter base. Enough to keep me busy once I do."

"See?" Kiera said. "That's called momentum. Now go enjoy obscene wealth for a few days."

The doorbell rang. "That's Mason," Jasmine said. "If I don't make it back, tell my story."

"I promise they will write about you in the history books. Go. And text me from the island." Kiera laughed. "Don't go anywhere alone with her."

Jasmine smiled, but for sure would keep to the buddy system where Brandy was concerned.

* * *

The private jet was... a lot.

Jasmine tried to act unimpressed, but the moment she sank into the plush leather seat and felt the plane lift smoothly into the air, she gave up pretending. Mason watched her with quiet amusement.

"Okay," she said, "this is incredible."

"Good," he said. "You deserve incredible."

The helicopter ride to the island somehow topped it. The doors were off, the wind whipping through her hair as turquoise water stretched endlessly below them. Jasmine laughed—really laughed—her fear and tension dissolving into exhilaration as Mason's hand found hers, grounding and warm. They landed on white sand and under impossibly blue skies. Tiffany was waiting. Brandy was not.

"She's on a call," Tiffany said dryly. "And hopefully that call will last exactly as long as it takes us to relax."

"Fingers crossed," Jasmine said.

Tiffany invited Jasmine to the spa. Mason declined. "I'm pretty enough thanks, enjoy ladies." he said.

They changed quickly and headed to the spa, the ocean breeze following them inside. Jasmine felt herself exhale for the first time in days.

The spa looked like something out of a five-star resort magazine.

Soft lighting glowed from recessed ceilings, casting a warm, golden hue over marble floors that reflected like glass. The air smelled faintly of eucalyptus, lavender, and something floral Jasmine couldn't name—but instantly felt calmer just breathing it in.

Plush white robes hung neatly on heated racks. Crystal pitchers filled with citrus-infused water lined a stone counter, next to neatly stacked, oversized towels that felt thicker than any blanket Jasmine owned.

Every surface whispered money.

Quiet luxury.

Women in sleek black uniforms moved through the space like they floated, speaking in low, soothing voices. Even their footsteps were soft.

Jasmine stood still for a moment, taking it all in.

She had never been this pampered. Never had people whose entire job was to make sure she was relaxed, hydrated, exfoliated, massaged, steamed, and glowing from head to toe.

"This place probably costs more than my first car," Jasmine murmured.

Tiffany smirked. "More than likely. Relax. You're with me. Today, you don't look at prices."

They were guided into private treatment rooms where heated tables waited, draped in crisp white linens. Warm towels were placed over Jasmine's shoulders. A woman with a gentle smile offered her herbal tea and asked about pressure preferences, skin sensitivities, stress levels—questions no one had ever asked her before. She'd never been to a spa before, not because she didn't want to but because the accountant in her thought it was a waste of money.

Being with Mason was its own reward. His love, his support, the safety she felt with him—that was priceless.

But Kiera was right.

The rich really did know how to live.

As she selected her treatments, Jasmine was taken immediately—no waiting, no lines. Just quiet efficiency and soft smiles.

Her massage came first. Warm oils, steady hands, and slow, deliberate movements worked tension out of muscles she hadn't even realized were tight. For once, her mind went blissfully blank.

Afterward, she was guided into a facial room where warm steam, gentle cleansers, and cool masks left her skin tingling and fresh. Someone tucked her in with a heated blanket and offered cucumber water like it was the most natural thing in the world.

Then came the soak.

She was led into a private room with a deep, stone tub filled with softly steaming water, petals floating on the surface and candles flickering along the edges. The water wrapped around her like silk.

That's where she rejoined Tiffany.

Tiffany was already there, eyes half-closed, looking just as relaxed as Jasmine felt.

"This is amazing," Jasmine murmured.

Tiffany smiled lazily. "Get used to it."

Jasmine leaned back, letting the warm water hold her.

As they soaked, Tiffany glanced over. "So, how's the business going?"

Jasmine smiled. "Better than I ever expected. Jeremy's been incredible—sent me clients, vouched for my work. I'm not officially open yet, but I've got a real foundation."

"That's amazing," Tiffany said, genuine envy flickering across her face. "I wish I could say the same."

Jasmine tilted her head. "Still no room to breathe?"

Tiffany sighed. "None. Mother oversees everything. Every decision. Even the ones that were originally mine."

"And yet," Jasmine said gently, "your ideas are making the company money."

"Millions. But credit doesn't equal control."

Jasmine hesitated, then said it anyway. "You could leave."

Tiffany smiled faintly. "Not this again. Bend over; is Mason's hand up there controlling you?"

Jasmine laughed. "Nope, not at the moment."

"Gross," Tiffany said. "But I can't. Not yet. This company is… everything. And Mother can't run it forever."

"That's a long time to wait," Jasmine said.

"I know. But when my chance comes, I'll be ready."

Jasmine nodded, understanding even if she didn't agree. "Just don't let waiting turn into disappearing."

Tiffany met her gaze. "I won't."

They sat in companionable silence after that, the ocean murmuring outside, the weight of expectation momentarily held at bay. Jasmine felt something like excitement settle in her chest. She was going to relax even if it killed her.

* * *

Mason waited until the house was empty.

Brandy had retreated to her room after a very awkward dinner with a phone call she clearly intended to stretch into the evening. Tiffany had disappeared toward the beach with a book and a drink, already sensing—wisely—that she was not meant to be part of whatever Mason had planned. He checked his watch once, then picked up the small box and slipped it into his pocket.

When Jasmine came downstairs, sun-kissed and relaxed from the spa, he was leaning casually against the doorframe. "Put on something comfortable," he said. "I'm stealing you."

Her brow lifted. "From paradise? What could be better than this?"

"You'll see."

That made her smile.

They walked a short distance before the road narrowed and ended. Beyond it was a path—worn smooth by time and footsteps—that led down toward the water. Mason took her hand and guided her forward, the air warm and fragrant with salt and flowering vines.

"Where are we going?" she asked.

"You'll see."

The path opened onto a secluded stretch of beach, untouched and quiet, framed by towering palms and the soft glow of the evening. At the far end, a small wooden pier extended over the water.

The sun was set. The waves rolled in gently, their rhythm steady and calming, as if the ocean itself was holding its breath for what was about to happen.

At the edge of the pier stood a flower arch, custom-built just for this moment. Cream, blush, and soft pink roses were woven together with eucalyptus and trailing greenery, the petals catching the breeze and releasing a faint, sweet scent into the air. Sheer white fabric draped from the arch, fluttering softly like whispers.

Candles lined the wooden planks of the pier, enclosed in glass lanterns so the wind couldn't touch them. Their warm glow reflected off the water, creating a pathway of light leading straight to the arch.

Every detail was intentional.

Every step forward felt like walking into a dream.

Soft music played quietly in the background—just loud enough to be heard over the waves, just soft enough to feel intimate. The air was warm, the moment suspended in time.

Jasmine stopped short. "Mason..."

He smiled, gentle and sure. "Come on."

They walked to the end of the pier, waves lapping softly below them. No one else was there. No noise. No expectations. Just sky, water, and the steady presence of the man beside her.

"This is beautiful," she whispered.

"It is," Mason said, turning to face her. "But that's not why I brought you here." Her heart stuttered. "I spent most of my life thinking love was something you managed. Negotiated. But with you,

I learned it's something you *choose*. Every day. When it's hard, when it's easy, and even when it snores loudly." Tears welled in her eyes and she chuckled as he took her hands. "You saw me clearly, and you stayed. Even when it was hard. Even when you were scared. I don't want a future that doesn't have you standing next to me—calling me out, grounding me, loving me."

He reached into his pocket and lowered himself onto one knee. Jasmine gasped, a hand flying to her mouth. "Jasmine Rayne Franklin," Mason said, voice steady but eyes bright, "will you marry me?"

For a moment, she couldn't speak. The world felt too big, too beautiful, too full.

"Yes," she finally said, breathless. "Yes, Mason." He slid the ring onto her finger—perfect, just like her—and stood, pulling her into his arms as she laughed and cried all at once. "I love you," she whispered into his chest.

"I've got you. Always."

They stayed wrapped around each other, the candles glowing brighter against the dark. Later, beneath a canopy of stars and back on the beach, they lay together on a blanket Mason had hidden away, the ocean murmuring close enough to feel alive. Their kisses were slow and intentional, their touches filled with reverence and joy.

Their love was patient, teasing, and sensual. Mason loved her like a promise kept—every touch asking, every response willing. Jasmine melted into him, unguarded and free, her laughter mixing with soft sighs as the night folded around them. They made love beneath the stars, skin warmed by salty air and trust, the future no longer something distant but something breathing between them.

* * *

The next morning felt like a gift. They toured the island on foot and by boat, meeting locals who welcomed them easily, stopping at markets and hidden beaches Mason insisted they explore.

They talked about everything and nothing—travel, careers, and the shape of the life they wanted to build.

At lunch, Mason leaned back in his chair and said casually, "So, ten kids?"

Jasmine nearly choked on her drink. "You're out of your mind."

"Six?"

"One," she said firmly.

He grinned. "Three."

She narrowed her eyes. "And a dog."

"Deal," Mason said instantly.

She laughed, slipping her hand into his, admiring the ring catching the sunlight. She was getting married!

* * *

The last dinner of the weekend tasted like obligation. Crystal glasses chimed softly against porcelain as the four of them sat together, the table heavy with food no one seemed eager to enjoy. Brandy presided at the head, her smile sharp and practiced, her comments sharpened even further.

"So soon," she said lightly, eyes flicking to Jasmine's hand. "One might think you're in a hurry."

Jasmine smiled back, sweet and unyielding. "When you know, you know."

Brandy hummed. "Of course. Though parentage often has a way of... shaping expectations."

Mason stiffened. Tiffany's jaw tightened. Jasmine met Brandy's gaze without blinking and said, "I can assure you I am not pregnant." The air crackled.

By the time dessert arrived, Mason had had enough. "That's it," he said flatly. "We're done for tonight."

Tiffany nodded, pushing back her chair. "Good night, Mother."

Brandy's smile didn't waver, but her eyes burned as she got up and stormed out of the room. Later, with the house finally quiet, Mason and Jasmine relaxed in the common living area, shoes discarded, tension slowly draining away. Mason handed her a large long box and a second, larger one.

"What's this?" she asked.

"Now that you're marrying me," he said with a grin, "you need a few outrageously bougie items." Inside was an engraved candlestick set and an elaborate vase—elegant, unnecessary, and undeniably beautiful.

Jasmine laughed. "You're ridiculous."

"And you love it." He kissed her forehead, and asked her to join him in the shower before bed. Jasmine giggled and told him she wanted to call Kiera and enjoy the night air a little longer. He Reminded her he'd let the staff go for the night and asking her to close the terrace doors and turn off the lights before bed. Then he disappeared down the hall.

Jasmine stepped out onto the terrace and called Kiera, the cool night air brushing against her skin as the sound of waves carried in the distance.

"I have been *loving* how you didn't send me any pictures I could be jealous of," Kiera said by way of greeting.

Jasmine laughed softly. "I've been a little busy..."

"Busy doing what?"

Jasmine lowered her voice, even though no one was near. "Getting engaged," she whispered loudly.

There was half a second of silence.

Then Kiera screamed.

"ENGAGED?!" Kiera shrieked so loudly Jasmine had to pull the phone away from her ear. "YOU'RE GETTING MARRIED?!"

"Yes!" Jasmine laughed. "We're getting married!"

"I knew it could happen!" Kiera rushed on, barely stopping to breathe. "I just didn't want to get my hopes up! Mason is such a great man! I can't wait to sell you both another house, your babies will be so—"

"Kiera," Jasmine cut in, laughing harder, "take a breath before you pass out."

Kiera inhaled dramatically. "Thank you. I'm lightheaded. I need to sit down."

There was a pause, like she actually did.

Then: "Okay. Tell me everything."

Jasmine smiled and told her about the beach, the flowers, the pier, the way Mason's hands had trembled just a little when he asked. She even told her about Brandy's less-than-warm reaction.

"I will come down there and slap the nice back into her," Kiera declared. "She will not mess up our moment."

Jasmine laughed. "We're happy, right?" Kiera asked, suddenly softer.

"So happy it's scary," Jasmine answered dreamily.

"Then you keep that glow," Kiera said. "She'll get over it."

They stayed on the phone, talking and laughing, while Jasmine leaned against the railing, watching the waves crash softly in the darkness.

Jasmine lingered even after her call was done. The night air was warm, the ocean dark and endless. She leaned against the terrace door. She was getting married. It felt like a dream. Until she heard footsteps.

Brandy stepped fully into the room. "You should enjoy the view," Brandy said, folding her arms as she surveyed the dark sea. "This phase of your life won't last long."

Jasmine didn't turn right away. "If you came in here to insult me again, you're wasting your breath."

A low laugh escaped Brandy. "You really are naïve. I didn't raise my son to marry a woman like you."

Jasmine faced her then. "You didn't raise him at all; the nannies did. You controlled him."

Brandy's smile thinned. "Control is love, darling. Something you wouldn't understand. Your father certainly didn't."

The word hit like a blade. "Don't," Jasmine said. "You don't get to talk about him."

"Oh, but I do." Brandy stepped closer, her voice mocking, sharpening. "Jack was a parasite. A liar who thought he could skate through life on charm and other people's money. Men like that don't live long."

"I agree my father was a bad man. That doesn't make his life any less valuable. After all, you're still breathing."

Brandy chuckled. "Wow, the kitten has claws. Who would have thought?"

"Listen, Brandy, I don't like you and you don't like me, but we both love Mason. Shouldn't that be enough?"

"Not at all, which is why I am willing to pay you one million dollars to disappear. You don't even need to pack. I can make all the ar—"

Jasmine cut her off. "Let me stop you there. I am not interested in your money."

"You sure? That's a lot of money. Anyone would jump at this chance."

"Are you so desperate to be in control that you're willing to make sure I am out of the picture? Mason knew who you were long before I came into his life. Even if I left, he'd never be who you want him to be. You are pathetic! Your own children don't even love you." Jasmine was so sick of this woman.

Brandy was seeing red; no one talked to her like this. "You don't know the first thing about my family, but I know all I need to know about you and yours. You think you'll ever be good enough? Your own father didn't want you—offered to sell you out for the same million dollars I'm offering you. His life was worthless, and so is yours."

Jasmine's chest tightened, so she turned and walked away from the terrace door, back into the living room. "He didn't deserve to die."

Brandy tilted her head. "He deserved to be gunned down like the trash he was."

Something cold crept into Jasmine's stomach. "What are you saying?"

"I'm saying that you have a choice, and the only one where you end up happy is a million dollars richer and some place far away from Mason."

"You sound crazy. Everyone knows I'm here. Even you aren't that stupid."

Brandy studied her face, clearly savoring the moment. "My husband spent years slowly killing himself just trying to keep up with me. Do you know how easy it is to help a weak heart along? A little stress. A little chemistry. The right doctor who asks no questions."

Jasmine felt dizzy. "You're lying."

"Am I?" Brandy's eyes glittered. "The police never questioned it. Why would they? A devoted wife. A grieving family. A spotless reputation."

Jasmine's voice shook. "And my father?"

Brandy's smile widened—cruel, unrepentant. "One gunshot. Clean. Efficient. Men like Jack collect enemies like debts. I simply... made sure it was paid."

Jasmine staggered back a step. "You murdered him."

Brandy shrugged. "Not me, dear. I'm a lady after all. *I* corrected a problem. I was hoping they'd think you did it with your rocky relationship. Unluckily for me, those idiots didn't even look your way."

Rage flared, burning through the shock. "You're sick."

Brandy's hand shot out then—fast, sharp. The slap echoed across the room, stinging Jasmine's cheek and ringing in her ears. "You listen to me," Brandy said through her teeth. "You will call off this engagement. You will walk away quietly. Or you will learn exactly how fragile life can be."

Jasmine's hands trembled, but she didn't look away. "You think Mason would ever forgive you if he knew?"

Brandy laughed softly. "Are you wearing a wire under that dress? Mason hates me. He always has, so no loss there. And even if he believed you—what proof would you have? A dead con man and a dead husband. And your word against mine? Please." She leaned in close. "Women like me don't get caught. We get what we want when we want it."

Something inside Jasmine broke—not fear, not grief, but fury. "You're a miserable, manipulative monster. Your husband was better off dead than trapped in a life with you."

Brandy straightened, eyes flashing. "Careful."

"No," Jasmine said, tears burning but unspilled. "You don't scare me anymore."

Brandy smiled then—slow, venomous. "I think your father said the same thing."

That was the moment. The moment Jasmine's hand closed around the heavy, engraved candlestick. And everything in her life changed forever. She didn't remember lifting it—only the sound, the impact, and the terrible finality as Brandy crumpled to the marble floor.

Silence.

"What I have done." Jasmine gasped dropping the candlestick.

"Oh no," said a voice. Jasmine spun to see Tiffany frozen in the doorway, horror etched across her face. "What have you done?"

"I—I didn't mean—" Jasmine dropped to her knees, hands shaking as she searched for a pulse that wasn't there. Blood spread beneath Brandy's head. "It was an accident. I swear."

Panic flooded in, thick and suffocating. Her life was over. Mason's life—ruined. There would be no proof of what Brandy had done, what she'd confessed to. Only this. Jasmine reached for her phone.

Tiffany stopped her. "Wait."

Jasmine got to her feet and waited for Tiffany to speak.

She wiped her eyes, voice unsteady but clear. "I heard everything. All of it." Jasmine froze. "My father," Tiffany whispered. "The doctors said heart attack. But ... our company produces drugs that could easily make things look like that. Your father..." Jasmine said nothing, afraid to breathe. "This was self-defense," Tiffany said, words tumbling out now. "She slapped you. She threatened you. I didn't move because I didn't know what to do. But I'm not letting her destroy anyone else's life."

"What are you saying—"

"We need a plan," Tiffany said fiercely.

Jasmine's heart was racing, she wanted this to be a dream. This could not be her life right now.

They stood quietly for a moment. Jasmine swallowed. "She can't just disappear."

"I know," Tiffany replied. "But she won't ruin Mason's life. Or yours."

The house felt too quiet, time suddenly fragile. Jasmine glanced at the clock—after one in the morning. Mason would be up early. She moved on instinct now, telling Tiffany to wait, checking the upstairs hallway, listening for any sign of movement. Nothing. She went upstairs to their door; the light was off and no sound came out. Back downstairs, she forced herself to think—not how to escape, but how to survive. Money made the world go round. Brandy had known that better than anyone.

Tiffany stood looking down at her mother when Jasmine returned. "He's still asleep."

Together, they moved Brandy's body out of sight, into the pool house closet. Hands slick with fear and resolve. Jasmine's mind raced, assembling possibilities without fully naming them. Tiffany sniffed, sad and thankful that she followed her mother downstairs. She thought at most she'd hide and tell Mason what happened just in case their mother tried lying.

Both of them in their own private prison as they thought about what they needed to do. Who they needed to be to get through this. Shared understanding. This wasn't justice. It was containment.

As the night stretched on, the first fragile outline of a story began to form—not perfect, not clean, but plausible enough to hold. And when Jasmine finally sat back, shaking and hollow, one thought echoed louder than all the rest: This secret would bind them forever. And it could cost them everything.

CHAPTER 12

Mason woke, reaching instinctively for Jasmine. Her side of the bed was cool, the sheets rumpled but empty. He rolled onto his back, blinking up at the ceiling before grabbing his phone from the nightstand; 7:36 a.m. He frowned. Jasmine never woke up early.

He pulled on a pair of shorts and headed out, following the faint sounds of movement until he found her in the kitchen. She stood barefoot at the island, curls loosely twisted up in a bun. She flipped something in a pan. Bacon sizzled. The smell alone made his stomach growl.

"Morning beautiful," he murmured.

She turned, smiling brightly, and he crossed the room to kiss her—slow, lingering, tasting coffee and something sweeter. "You know we have staff for this," he said against her lips.

She giggled. "I like cooking. And I gave them the morning off."

He frowned, stealing a strip of bacon from the plate. "This is a vacation. That's literally what we pay them for."

She swatted at his hand, laughing as he crunched happily and went to the fridge for juice. "Go shower. Breakfast will be ready soon."

He eyed the growing spread. "I'll be right back."

By the time he returned, the kitchen looked like a magazine spread—eggs, pancakes, bacon piled high, pastries and muffins arranged neatly, and an assortment of juices lined up like a tasting flight.

But Jasmine wasn't there. He heard her voice instead. It came from the terrace—low, tense, nothing like the light tone she'd used minutes earlier. He moved toward the sound, careful not to interrupt, catching the tail end of the conversation.

"I don't care about the cost," she whispered. "You're in. Make it happen."

She ended the call—smiling instantly when she saw him, like flipping a switch. "Work stuff," she said easily. "Everything's done. Dig in."

He studied her for a half-second too long, then shook it off and took her hand, leading her back inside. "You cooked. I'll dish the plates."

She smiled, relieved. "Deal."

They'd just taken a few bites when Tiffany wandered in, already dressed for the day, big sunglasses covering her eyes.

"Where's Sammy?" she asked, stopping at the island. "I just want a veggie omelet."

Mason smirked and pointed his fork at Jasmine. "Meet Chef Jasmine. Staff's off this morning."

Jasmine gave an apologetic smile. "Sorry."

Tiffany winced. "You will be when Mother comes down. She only eats eggs Benedict in the morning. She's going to lose it."

"It's fine," Jasmine said quickly. "She was already up and left." Mason looked at her, confused. "She was … angry," Jasmine added, smoothing her napkin unnecessarily. "When I told her I let the staff go. Said a few not-so-nice things. Then she left." Mason sighed, rubbing his temple. Tiffany nodded.

Tiffany muttered. "Thank God this is our last day." She grabbed a muffin and a juice. "I've got tennis in an hour. See you later." Her eyes lingered on Jasmine for a second. Jasmine nodded, almost indiscernibly. When Tiffany left, the kitchen fell quiet again.

Mason reached for Jasmine's hand. "Hey." She looked at him, eyes a little too bright, smile just a little too careful. "You okay?" he asked.

She nodded. "Yeah. Just … ready to go home."

He squeezed her fingers. "Me too."

Outside, the island glittered under the sun—beautiful, untouched, and utterly unaware of how much had already shifted beneath its calm surface.

Jasmine finished her mimosa and set the glass aside, eyes alight with purpose.

"I want to go on that boat tour."

Mason didn't even look up from his coffee. "No."

She blinked. "Excuse you?"

"I told you yesterday—it's too hot. You'll be miserable."

She slid closer, tugged gently on his arm, and deployed the full force of her puppy-dog eyes. "I know. But I'm a tourist. And I really want to do it."

He studied her, unimpressed. "You hate heat. You complain after ten minutes."

"You don't have to go with me," she added quickly. "It's just a few hours. I'll be fine."

That gave him pause. "And you're sure I can trust you to entertain yourself without setting something on fire?"

She grinned. "I make no promises—but yes."

He sighed, defeated. "Fine. I'll drop you off."

She kissed his cheek. "Thank you."

Mason dropped her at the marina an hour later, watching until she disappeared down the dock before heading off to get his hair trimmed and knock out a few errands before their flight. While paying for a box of imported cigars, he called his mother. Voicemail. He frowned and dialed Tiffany instead.

"I'll probably catch a plane with you guys," Tiffany said. "I called Mother too—she texted that she was busy and would talk to me later."

Mason shrugged it off. "She's pouting because we didn't let her bully Jasmine at dinner."

Once Jasmine texted that she was ready, Mason headed back. When they returned to the house, Sammy was plating lunch while Tiffany sat at the island, scrolling her phone.

"Will Mother be joining us?" Mason asked politely.

"I haven't seen her," Tiffany replied, frowning.

Mason sighed. "I'll go check if the queen plans to grace us with her presence."

Brandy's room was pristine—bed made, closet full, but no sign of her. Back in the kitchen, Mason asked Sammy, "Have you seen our mother?"

Sammy said. "Greg said he saw her grab a few things and leave with a man."

Tiffany snorted. "Of course she did." Greg was summoned—and arrived, sweating a little. "Why are you sweating like that?" Tiffany asked. "Ew."

"I believe I am getting sick," Greg said, eyes wide.

"Gross," Tiffany muttered. "Do not touch my things."

Jasmine nudged Mason sharply. He sighed. "Greg, you should go home."

"No, Mister Jewel—"

"Paid leave," Mason added.

Greg nodded rapidly and fled.

Lunch was served—grilled mahi-mahi, citrus salad, warm bread. Tiffany pretended to get a text. "Oh good," she said theatrically. "Mother says to leave without her."

Mason shrugged. "Maybe getting laid will make her less bitchy."

Tiffany smirked. "Unlikely. But she does find a lover down here often."

Soon, it was time to leave. On the helicopter ride, Mason noticed Jasmine's exhaustion immediately. "I told you the sun would wipe you out."

She frowned and looked away. "Thanks. Exactly what I wanted to hear."

He chuckled softly and took her hand, stilling her restless fingers. "You know what I mean."

At the airport lounge, she seemed distracted. "I'm just switching out of vacation mode," she said. "Thinking about everything waiting at home."

He nodded. "Business going good?"

Her face lit up, he knew that would get a smile out of her. She talked excitedly about clients, plans, and timelines, but he could see something was off. Maybe bringing her here and subjecting her to Brandy wasn't a good idea. After they were married, he would limit their interactions—his as well; he was happy and Brandy would not take this from him. Jasmine brought him peace, love, and other feelings he'd never felt before. She was it for him.

"I think I can put in my notice soon," she said. "Maybe open the office in a few months."

He kissed her knuckles. "I'm proud of you. Just promise me you'll hire a wedding planner. I don't want to wait a year or more to make you my wife."

She laughed. "Deal."

They talked dates, venues—dreams unfolding easily between them. Then it was time to board, heading home together, unaware of how fragile everything truly was.

* * *

Mason pulled up in front of Jasmine's place and cut the engine, turning to her with an easy smile.

"Grab whatever you need. I want you to stay over for a while," he said. "Meet me at my place when you're done?"

She leaned over and kissed him, soft and lingering. "I promise. I won't be long."

"We need to talk about you getting moved in."

"Hold your horses, tiger. Who says we're staying at that monstrosity you call a house?"

"You don't like my house?"

"It's great, but I would like something we both love that's a little homier."

"I can get behind that."

She kissed him and got out the car. He watched until she disappeared inside before driving away, the familiar comfort of routine settling over him as he headed home. Once there, he dropped his luggage straight into the laundry room—his maid would handle it—then went to his office, loosening his collar as he powered up his computer.

Before diving into emails, he hesitated and picked up his phone. He called his mother. Voicemail. Again. Mason frowned. That wasn't like Brandy. Angry, vindictive, passive-aggressive—yes. Silent? Never. She confronted conflict like a sport, head-on and unapologetic. He tried once more. Nothing. Unease crept in, subtle but persistent. He dialed Sammy.

"Mister Jewel," Sammy answered promptly.

"Is my mother still there?" Mason asked.

"No, sir," Sammy replied. "She texted earlier asking me to pack her belongings. Then again when she was outside. Michael loaded her luggage into her trunk about thirty minutes ago."

Mason exhaled slowly. "Thank you, Sammy."

He hung up and leaned back in his chair, shaking his head. She was taking the engagement harder than he thought. The idea made him smile a little. The wedding would send her into a full tailspin. A Jewel marrying someone without equal—or greater—status? It probably felt like poison to her. Still, she'd plaster on a smile for her two-faced friends and pretend to approve. The image made him chuckle quietly.

An hour later, his phone rang; "Tiffany" flashed across the screen. "Hey—"

"Mason," Tiffany's voice cut in, sharp and frantic. "There's been an accident. With Mother." The room tilted. "They're saying … I don't even know yet. They just—Mason, they need us back on the island. Now."

Time fractured.

He was suddenly standing in a hospital hallway, fluorescent lights buzzing overhead, the air smelling like antiseptic and dread. People rushed past him, blurring together, while he stood frozen—exactly like the day his father died.

"Mason!"

Tiffany's voice snapped him back.

"We sent the jet back already," he said, his own voice sounding distant to his ears. "I'll call and have it turned around. You check commercial flights—whatever's fastest."

"Okay," Tiffany said breathlessly and ended the call.

Mason felt himself pulled back into the past. He thought about the days after his father died.

His days felt muted. Like someone had turned the volume down on the world.

He moved through those first few weeks like a ghost, wandering from room to room in a house that suddenly felt too big. Too quiet. Nothing felt real. People came and went—offering condolences, shaking his hand, telling him how strong he was—but their voices sounded distant, like they were underwater.

The pain was unlike anything he had ever felt. It was heavy.

A constant, crushing weight in his chest that made it hard to breathe.

Tiffany cried almost nonstop. He would hear her in her room late at night, muffling her sobs into a pillow. During the day she tried to hold it together, but her eyes stayed swollen and red. She had always been strong, but grief made her small for a while.

Brandy barked orders.

Funeral arrangements. Business calls. Estate meetings. Image management. She moved through it all like a general commanding troops, refusing to crumble. Mason couldn't tell if she was being strong—or if she simply didn't know how to mourn without losing control.

His father had been his anchor. His sounding board. His quiet strength. When Brandy's expectations suffocated, when life felt overwhelming—his father had been steady ground. Now that ground was gone.

There were nights he would reach for his phone to call his father before remembering.

It took months before the fog began to thin. Even then, it never fully lifted.

When his father died, it had felt like the earth split open beneath his feet. Like the foundation of his life had been ripped away without warning.

This felt like standing in a room waiting for news about a stranger.

He understood the gravity of it. He knew what it meant. If Brandy was truly gone, it would shift the entire structure of his world. The company. The family name. The expectations. The tension that had always lived just beneath his skin.

But emotionally? There was no collapse. No suffocating weight on his chest.

No desperate urge to hear her voice one last time. Just sadness and uncertainty and that unsettled him.

Because whether she had loved him well or not... she was still his mother.

He wondered if something inside him had shut down years ago. If the constant maneuvering, the manipulation, the conditional affection had slowly cauterized whatever bond had once been there.

Or maybe he had simply learned how to survive without her long before he ever had to lose her.

Either way, the absence of devastation felt like its own kind of loss.

Mason stared at his phone, disbelief pounding through him. Not again. This couldn't be happening again. He scrolled and pressed Jasmine's name. As the phone rang, one thought echoed relentlessly in his mind: Everything had just changed.

* * *

Tiffany hung up the phone in tears. This was not how this was supposed to happen.

Her stomach twisted violently, and she barely made it to the bathroom before dropping to her knees and emptying what little she'd eaten for lunch. When it was over, she sat back against the cool tile, shaking.

The plans were in place. There was no turning back now.

She felt sick—not just physically, but morally.

She wanted not to care. She wanted to harden her heart and remind herself that this woman had destroyed her life. Had taken her favorite person in the world from her.

Her father had believed in her. Encouraged her. Told her she could be anything she wanted to be. He praised everything about her—even the stubbornness, even the fire.

He had loved her without conditions. And now she knew.

Her mother had made it happen.

Two deaths Brandy had confessed to. But Tiffany knew in her bones there were more. Women like her didn't stop at two. Power didn't satisfy itself neatly. It grew hungry.

The lie she and Jasmine were now living inside was something Tiffany never imagined she would be capable of. Manipulation she was use to. Deception of this level she was not. The performance they would both need to sell.

But there was no way—no way—she would let Jasmine rot in jail while Brandy rested peacefully in a grave, having ruined one more life on her way out.

She had known Jasmine would change Mason's life. She had never imagined she would unearth something this big. Something this ugly.

Tiffany pushed herself up off the floor, splashed cold water on her face, and stared at her reflection. This was bigger than grief now.

She called her driver. She needed to get to the airport—and she was in no condition to drive.

As she walked out the door, one thought echoed in her mind: She was in charge now and things were about to change.

CHAPTER 13

Jasmine sat on the edge of her couch, phone cradled loosely in her hands, the screen dark. Twenty-four hours ago, her biggest concern had been wedding dates and guest lists. She had been blissfully happy—engaged, loved, safe. Now she was no where near safe.

Her mind replayed the moment over and over, cruel and relentless. If she'd said something different. If she'd walked away. If she'd swallowed the insults. Any version of the night that hadn't ended with Brandy Jewel's blood on marble and Jasmine's hands shaking with the aftermath.

She closed her eyes. Her father's voice rose unbidden, a memory she'd spent years trying to bury. *Everyone has a price, Jas. Even the ones who swear they don't.* She had hated him for saying it. Now she understood. The cost of keeping Mason—the man she loved more than anything—was this. Silence. Complicity. Blood money. And the knowledge that she was no better than the man she'd spent her life running from. A murderer was a murderer, no matter the reason. Her stomach twisted as the flashback took hold.

. . .

They hadn't spoken much as they worked. Shock had made everything surreal—like watching herself move from far away. Tiffany had been frighteningly composed, as had she, issuing instructions in clipped, efficient sentences, while Jasmine focused on restoring the room to order. Cleaning the candlestick. No bloodstains. No sign that anything irreversible had happened.

They hid Brandy's body in the pool house closet, wrapped and weighted with grim efficiency. Jasmine scrubbed the living room floor until her arms ached, until the space looked exactly as it had hours earlier—perfect, pristine, untouched. A lie, polished to shine.

When it was done, Jasmine knew one thing with terrifying clarity: they couldn't do this alone. She called Greg one of the butlers. Her father had taught her many terrible things, but one lesson had stuck: *people tell you who they are if you pay attention.*

Greg didn't like this family. That much had always been obvious to her. He tolerated them for the paycheck, the long hours and quiet resentment simmering just beneath his politeness. And resentment, she knew, was fertile ground.

He hesitated when she explained she needed help for money no questions asked—voice tight, fear threading through every word. But fear could be managed. Money was easier. The number Tiffany offered made him go quiet. It was more than he'd ever hoped to have in one lifetime. Enough to stop living paycheck to paycheck. Enough to fight for custody of his son he'd said. Enough to change his life.

Tiffany watched him closely, eyes cold. "And if you mess this up," Tiffany said calmly, "you take the fall. Every bit of it. I'll make sure of that." Jasmine winced at the cruelty—but it worked. Greg nodded. Later, Tiffany pushed further. She had to. She told him they needed a story that didn't invite questions. Something tragic. Something no one would want to examine too closely.

Greg mentioned a friend—or rather, his friend's son. Someone adjacent enough to be useful, desperate enough to listen, and greedy enough to accept what was offered without asking for details. The rest was handled in murmurs and implications. Instructions spoken aloud. No specifics written down. Only understanding. Only money changing hands. Only silence.

Now, alone again, Jasmine stared at her phone as it buzzed softly in her hand. *Mason*. Her breath caught painfully in her chest. This was the moment she'd been dreading. The moment where she'd either lose him—or doom him along with her.

She answered. "Mason?"

His voice sounded strained. "Jasmine ... there's been an accident. With my mother."

The room spun. She closed her eyes, steadying herself against the onslaught of guilt and terror and something darker—relief she hated herself for feeling. "I—I'm so sorry," she whispered, it wasn't a lie.

As she listened to him speak, one thought echoed louder than the rest, relentless and damning: she had crossed a line she could never uncross. And no amount of love—not even Mason's—would ever make her innocent again. She would carry this burden alone, without him. She knew with Tiffany backing her she could get him to understand, but this was one emotion she would not force him to experience. It was bad enough Tiffany had to be involved.

He spoke, voice tight, controlled in a way that told her everything was not. "I need you to meet me at the airport. Now."

"I'll be there," she said immediately. "Thirty minutes."

Her hands were already shaking as she grabbed her keys and rushed out the door. The drive was a blur of red lights and whispered prayers—for forgiveness, not for Brandy but for Tiffany and herself. For silence. For everything to go exactly as planned. At the airport, time dragged cruelly. Forty minutes to wait for the jet to return and refuel felt like forty hours. Inside the cabin, the air was thick with tension.

Tiffany was unraveling—tears streaking down her face one moment, rage flashing the next. Mason sat rigid beside Jasmine, jaw tight, gaze fixed on nothing. He was holding it together. Jasmine watched them both, her chest aching with remorse. Not for Brandy. For *them*.

They had loved her—however complicated that love was. They had memories, history, a family shaped by her presence. Jasmine had taken something from them that could never be replaced. That was the weight she carried now. But Jasmine had had what Tiffany never did—a mother who loved without condition, a family who protected her not because of obligation or power, but because of affection.

Jasmine deserved happiness. She deserved a future with Mason. Children. A life untouched by manipulation and fear. Mason could never know what his mother had said. What she had confessed. Who she had *been*. The world was quieter without her.

When they landed, everything moved fast—security, cars waiting, sirens cutting through the air. They were taken straight to the hospital, then ushered into a sterile conference room that smelled faintly of disinfectant and grief. A uniformed officer spoke gently but plainly. Witnesses had reported hearing a loud explosion before the helicopter fell from the sky into the water. Emergency responders arrived quickly, but there was nothing to be done. The wreckage had sunk fast. They recovered what they could of Brandy Jewel's body. The pilot's was still missing. Divers were searching but officers weren't hopeful.

"We are sorry for your loss," the officer said.

Jasmine squeezed Mason's hand. He didn't look at her—just stared ahead, eyes unfocused. Tiffany broke down completely, sobbing one moment, then suddenly lashing out about lawsuits and negligence, about how the company would pay. She played her role well. Too well. Jasmine turned to Mason quietly. "How are you?"

He exhaled slowly, like he'd been holding his breath for years. "I don't know. Part of me is sad. Another part ... feels relieved. And that makes me feel like a terrible person."

"I know it all too well. I felt the same about Jack."

He swallowed hard. "She caused so much damage. So much pain. But she was still my mother." Jasmine leaned closer, resting her head against his shoulder and spoke. "My mother used to say that parents are just people. Flawed, broken, doing the best they can—or not. And it's okay to grieve what they were *supposed* to be, not just what they were." She closed her eyes. "Maybe that's what this is. Grieving the idea of her. Letting go of the damage."

Jasmine held his hand tighter, heart heavy and resolute. Some truths would remain buried.

* * *

Brandy's funeral was everything she would have loved. The chapel was full—overflowing, really—with people eager to tell stories about her strength, her influence, her generosity. Every word spoken about her was reverent, polished, and careful. Jasmine listened from her seat. Her gaze swept around, taking in the crowd, and she felt a strange disconnect settle in her chest. This didn't feel real.

Mason squeezed her hand, grounding her. She turned to look at him. His face was composed, grief present but restrained—he was taking her death better than Jasmine had expected. Better than she had feared. The sight eased her guilt, if only a little.

She told herself—over and over—that Brandy would have had her killed if she hadn't acted first. Just like she had Mason's father. Just like she had Jasmine's. The truth burned in her throat, begging to be released. She wanted to tell Mason so badly, to unburden herself, to make him understand why things had unfolded the way they had. But she wouldn't do that to him.

She wanted to tell Kiera, but she couldn't make her friend take something like that on either. Tiffany already knew. She knew exactly what kind of monster her mother had been, and she would carry that knowledge for the rest of her life. Jasmine couldn't place that weight on Mason too. Loving Brandy as a mother was complicated enough—loving her while knowing the truth would destroy him. He'd told Jasmine about his parents' last interaction, how his father had tried to leave. Brandy had made sure he left, but on her terms.

Then the funeral was over, and they stood, receiving last respects. One person after another approached Mason to offer condolences, then Tiffany, who stood directly to his left. The line never seemed to end. Jasmine watched faces blur together—politicians, socialites, business associates—many of them people she was certain hadn't shed a single tear. Some were there to grieve. Others were there to be seen.

At one point, someone had the audacity to ask Mason and Tiffany to pose for a photo. They'd been swiftly escorted out, the moment handled quietly but firmly. As the service ended, Jasmine felt two opposing emotions settle side by side in her chest: grief and relief. She no longer had to look over her shoulder. No longer had to wonder when the other shoe would drop, when another threat would surface wrapped in politeness and power.

She was free—from her father, from Brandy, from the constant shadow of danger. And whether Mason ever knew it or not, he was free too. Jasmine tightened her grip on his hand, choosing silence, choosing love, choosing peace. Some truths, she knew, were meant to be buried.

EPILOGUE

Jasmine
Two years later

Jasmine stood in the doorway of her office and smiled. The sign on the glass read "Franklin Accounting and Forensic Audits," clean and understated. Inside, sunlight spilled across polished wood floors, shelves lined with neatly labeled files and books, framed degrees, and two single photographs on her desk—her mother, young and laughing, frozen in a moment before life hardened. The other was of Mason and Jasmine on their wedding day, smiling and in love.

The business was thriving quietly, honestly, and on its own merit. Jeremy Billups had been only the beginning. Word of mouth had done the rest. Wealthy clients valued discretion. Corporations valued accuracy. Jasmine had built a reputation that couldn't be bought or bullied—only earned. Every case she took, every account she balanced, felt like a small act of redemption. A way of proving—to herself most of all—that she was not her father, and she never would be.

At night, the nightmares came less often now. Mason chalked it up to her losing her father. If only it was that simple. Therapy had helped. Not miracles, but tools. Language for grief she'd never be allowed to name. A place to mourn her father honestly—not the man he was at his worst, but the broken human being who had loved her in his own inadequate way. A place to finally say goodbye.

Mason waited for her in the car the first couple of times she went, scrolling through emails he pretended not to care about anymore. Jewel Pharmaceuticals had changed under Tiffany's leadership. She had outlived her mother's shadow, not by fleeing it, but by reshaping it. The board respected her. The company thrived. And Brandy Jewel —once so loud, so domineering—had faded into a carefully curated memory. An accident. A tragedy. A closed case. The world had moved on. Mason had too.

He still carried his parents with him—his father's steady moral compass, his mother's cautionary absence. Therapy had taught him something essential: love wasn't required to hurt. You could acknowledge what hurt you without letting it define you. And Jasmine—Jasmine was his future. They married on a quiet stretch of coastline, with just the people who mattered most. No spectacle. No press. Tiffany and Kiera cried harder than anyone else.

Jasmine laughed when she remembered she'd told Mason to stop bugging her and they'd settled on three kids and a dog—*eventually*. She rubbed her softly rounded belly and shook her head; that man always got what he wanted.

Sometimes, late at night, when the house was quiet and the wind whispered through the trees, Jasmine would sit beside Mason and think about the choices that had brought them here. About the line she had crossed and the price she would always carry. She wasn't innocent, but she was honest now. And maybe that was enough.

Because life, she had learned, wasn't about erasing the past. It was about deciding what kind of future you'd build in its wake. She chose love. And he chose her.

* * *

Tiffany shut the door to her office, the soft click echoing in the quiet space. Outside, the nameplate read "Tiffany Jewel, CEO" —a title she'd worked her entire life toward, though not in the way she'd imagined. She sank into her chair after yet another meeting, exhaustion settling deep in her bones. This was what she'd wanted. Power. Autonomy. Respect. But it wasn't how she'd wanted to get here.

Two years ago, she'd stood frozen outside another door—the one where Jasmine and Brandy had been arguing. Shame still curled in her stomach when she thought about it. Hearing her mother calmly offer to *pay* Jasmine to leave Mason had shaken her, but nothing could have prepared her for what followed. The conversation had shifted—fast, violent, irreversible. Her mother had murdered her father.

He had been a good man, and an even better father. Where Brandy had been indifferent, he had been present—gentle, engaged, and loving in ways that mattered. Tiffany had always assumed that once Mason turned eighteen, her parents would quietly divorce. They didn't love each other. That much had been obvious.

Her father had fallen in love with someone else. Tiffany had found the text messages on his phone when she was sixteen. She knew about the open marriage, about the constant arguments—more than Mason ever had. And when her father died of a so-called "heart attack," she'd believed it. Or at least, she'd accepted it. Never—not in a million years —had she imagined her mother capable of killing him.

She wondered often what had pushed Brandy to do it. Fear? Rage? Control? Now that her mother was dead, she would never know. The answers were buried with her. As far as Tiffany was concerned, justice had been served. She wished she hadn't witnessed it. The memory still haunted her. But it was good that she *knew*. She'd let therapy handle the rest.

Without seeing the truth with her own eyes, she never would have believed Jasmine. And Jasmine had needed her—desperately. None of this would've been possible without her. In the aftermath, Tiffany and Jasmine had grown close. Real close. They spent time together—dinners, late nights, quiet conversations that felt honest and unguarded. She even liked Jasmine's friend Kiera a lot. Sometimes Tiffany and Kiera went out without Jasmine.

She'd never had real friends before. Not people who didn't care about her money. Not people unafraid to call her out on her mess. She wouldn't end up like her mother—cold, manipulative, hollow. Tiffany would lead with integrity. With honor. And yes—maybe a little yelling, because she was still herself. She was changing. Growing. But she was still Tiffany.

She traveled more now, trusting her second-in-command to keep things running. For the first time, she wasn't micromanaging out of fear. She was living. And soon, she'd be an aunt. The thought made her smile. She couldn't wait to spoil the little crumb-snatcher rotten. She was more open to love these days. Less concerned with status, appearances, and pedigree. She had money—plenty of it—and now she understood that money didn't make love.

What Jasmine had done… it was unthinkable and extraordinary all at once. Their mother had killed their father. She'd threatened to kill Jasmine too. And Jasmine—who had every reason to walk away—had stayed. She'd loved Mason enough to carry a secret she'd never asked for. Protected him, even when she didn't have to. That kind of love changed people. Tiffany leaned back in her chair, staring at the ceiling. One day, she hoped to find someone who would love her through the hard times too.

* * *

Mason closed his computer and pressed the intercom.

"Yes, Mr. Jewel?"

"I'm done for the day. Please reschedule my two o'clock."

"Yes, Mr. Jewel. Have a good night—and say hi to Jasmine for me."

"Will do. Have a good night, Sheila."

Mason stood, already smiling. He was leaving early, and for once, it wasn't for business. Jasmine had her ultrasound today—the one where they'd find out the sex of the baby. Mason didn't care what the results were. Boy or girl, he just wanted to know who the little person was that tapped gentle reminders against Jasmine's belly, as if saying, *I'm here.*

He hadn't known happiness could feel this steady. Two short years ago, he'd been mourning his mother after the helicopter she was in malfunction, killing her. Relief tangled with grief. Acceptance with disappointment. He'd made peace with the fact that she would never become the mother he needed her to be. Therapy had helped. More than he'd ever admit out loud.

Jasmine still went too. The nightmares came less often now, but sometimes stress brought them back—just like his dreams of his father did. Healing, he'd learned, wasn't linear. As Mason drove home, he marveled at the life he was living. He and Tiffany were closer than ever. She came over for dinner regularly, along with Tank, Terrence, Ebony, and Kiera. They'd become a family—not by obligation, but by choice.

Their new house was smaller than his old one, but every space felt warm and intentional. Jasmine had seen to that. Tiffany and Jasmine had grown especially close after Brandy's death, and Mason knew losing their mother had freed Tiffany to finally become herself.

He barely recognized the man he was now—in the best way. Fewer meetings. More poker nights. Plans to take three months of paternity leave once the baby arrived.

Pulling into the driveway, Mason smiled. Once inside, he called out, "Jasmine?"

"In here." He followed the sound to the kitchen, where she stood glowing in a way that had nothing to do with the afternoon light. He kissed her, then bent to press a gentle kiss to her belly. "What are you doing home?" she asked, smiling. "I thought you were meeting me at the doctor's office."

"I couldn't wait," he said. "Let's go now."

"Mason," she said, laughing. "Our appointment isn't until four."

"So? We pay them a lot of money."

She shook her head, amused, and stepped closer. "I know something that can keep you occupied until it's time to go."

She took his hand and led him upstairs. Pregnancy had awakened something fierce and playful in Jasmine, and Mason loved every second of it. They took their time, rediscovering each other in quiet, familiar ways. Mason adored the changes in her body, the softness, the strength, the life growing beneath his hand.

* * *

When they sat at the appointment together, calm and smiling, the anticipation returned—stronger than before. Soon, they'd know who was joining their world, and Mason had never felt more ready. He sat back, grinning up at the ultrasound screen as if it were the most beautiful thing he'd ever seen.

"A healthy baby boy," the doctor said with a smile.

Mason didn't even try to contain himself. "A boy?" he shouted, laughter and disbelief colliding in his chest. "We're having a boy!"

Jasmine laughed, shaking her head at him, eyes bright. "You are *so* dramatic."

"Mason the Third," he said instantly. "Trey, for short."

She laughed harder, but she didn't say no. He FaceTimed Tiffany before the gel was even wiped from Jasmine's stomach. Then Tank. By the time he was halfway through calling Terrance, Jasmine gently nudged him. "Can you get off the phone and let the doctor finish?" He complied—barely—but not before texting everyone to come over that night to celebrate.

The house filled quickly. Tiffany arrived first, already planning baby outfits. Kiera followed with dessert. Tank and Terrance came loud and smiling, Ebony right beside Terrance, beaming. They ate, talked, laughed—stories overlapping, plans forming—until Jasmine finally yawned, stretched, and politely put everyone out. Now the house was quiet again.

Mason lay in bed with the bedside lamp on, staring at the ultrasound while Jasmine slept beside him, her breathing soft and even. One hand rested protectively over her belly. He was going to be a father. Not the kind who delegated everything to a team of nannies. Jasmine had already planned to take three months off, and after that, she'd have a nanny on-site at her office—one of the perks of being the owner. Mason planned to be just as present. He wanted to be the kind of father his own had been—loving, available, steady.

There would be scraped knees and late-night feedings. First words. First heartbreaks. And he intended to be there for all of it. He turned his head, watching Jasmine sleep. This woman was it for him. He loved her strength. Her bravery. Her intelligence. Her beauty—inside and out—was unmatched. It hadn't been easy getting here. They'd fought for this life, earning every ounce of peace they now held. But nothing worth having ever came easy. This was the family he was building. And Mason knew, without a single doubt, that he wouldn't change any of it for the world. This was the woman he chose.

ACKNOWLEDGMENTS

First and foremost, to God, whom I am nothing without—I give You all the glory. Thank You for my dreams, creativity, strength, and for carrying me through every step of this process. This book exists because of Your grace and guidance.

To my husband, Tre—my best friend and my biggest supporter—thank you for listening to all my ideas, believing in me, and encouraging me even when I doubted myself. I love you more than words can say.

To my beautiful daughters, Leah and Kori, you are my heart. I hope you always remember that with God on your side, nothing is out of your reach. Dream big, believe in yourselves, and never be afraid to go after what you want.

To my dream team—my mother, Samone, Toya (my amazing beta reader), Tiera, and Nikki—thank you for your constant support, honesty, and for always being my cheerleaders. I truly could not have done this without you.

There are so many people who have supported and encouraged me along this journey, and while I don't have room to name everyone, please know how deeply grateful I am. A special thank you to Darlene, James, Monique, Judy, Jeff, Steven, and Leslie—and to everyone else who lifted me up along the way. I love and appreciate you all more than you know.

To my readers—thank you for taking this journey with me. I am nervous and all types of excited to hear how you guys feel about Mason and Jasmines story. And dare I say Tiffany could be next?! Buckle up, buttercup—this is where it gets fun!

www.ingramcontent.com/pod-product-compliance
Ingram Content Group UK Ltd.
Pitfield, Milton Keynes, MK11 3LW, UK
UKHW022003190726
13853UKWH00004B/1695